"Cathy, one little

"Yes?" She smiled politely.

"Why do you always wear your hair pulled back like that?"

"Because I like it that way, Steve."

"Oh," he said dryly as he stooped over her. "Your hair smells wonderful."

Suspiciously, she retorted, "I just washed it."

"Well, I like it down much better."

Cathy felt the two small combs at the back of her head being pulled out and her hair falling in disarray around her shoulders.

"Steve Bronsky! First you tell me where I'm going to sleep and now you want to tell me how to fix my hair!" She jumped up from the sofa and shoved him aside. "I'm getting out of here. Now."

"Please Cathy...you can't just walk out on me," he pleaded.

"Watch me!"

Dear Reader:

Romance offers us all so much. It makes us "walk on sunshine." It gives us hope. It takes us out of our own lives, encouraging us to reach out to others. Janet Dailey is fond of saying that romance is a state of mind, that it could happen anywhere. Yet nowhere does romance seem to be as good as when it happens *here*.

Starting in February 1986, Silhouette Special Edition will feature the AMERICAN TRIBUTE—a tribute to America, where romance has never been so wonderful. For six consecutive months, one out of every six Special Editions will be an episode in the AMERICAN TRIBUTE, a portrait of the lives of six women, all from Oklahoma. Look for the first book, *Love's Haunting Refrain* by Ada Steward, as well as stories by other favorites—Jeanne Stephens, Gena Dalton, Elaine Camp and Renee Roszel. You'll know the AMERICAN TRIBUTE by its patriotic stripe under the Silhouette Special Edition border.

AMERICAN TRIBUTE—six women, six stories, starting in February.

AMERICAN TRIBUTE—one of the reasons Silhouette Special Edition is just that—Special.

The Editors at Silhouette Books

ALIDA WALSH
This Business of Love

Silhouette Special Edition

Published by Silhouette Books New York

America's Publisher of Contemporary Romance

SILHOUETTE BOOKS
300 E. 42nd St., New York, N.Y. 10017

Copyright © 1985 by Alida Walsh

Distributed by Pocket Books

ISBN: 0-373-09273-3

First Silhouette Books printing November 1985

10 9 8 7 6 5 4 3 2 1

America's Publisher of Contemporary Romance

Printed in the U.S.A.

ALIDA WALSH

has added writing to an already enviable and varied career. Her accomplishments have included: being an Air Force cryptographer, a producer-director for educational TV and a language professor in a Florida university.

Alida is an accomplished gardener and raises orchids and Beveren rabbits on her land in Clearwater, Florida.

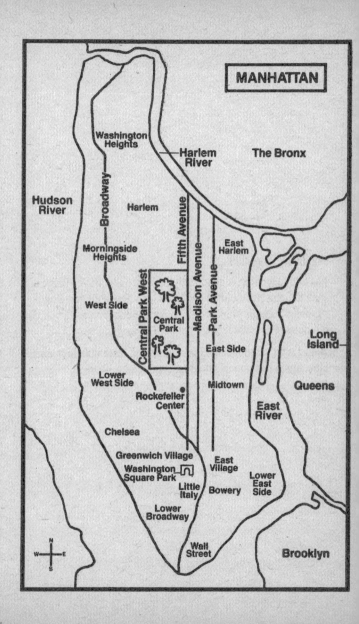

Chapter One

An unnatural quiet settled over the dimly lit bedroom, a silence disturbed only by the soft rustling of satin sheets. The auburn-haired woman snuggled into the arms of the man lying next to her, her green eyes glowing with satisfaction, her lips forming a complacent smile.

Slowly, his large hand brushed across her bare arm. "I've dreamed about this a hundred times"—his face and voice were expressionless as he went on—"but I never thought it would happen." And then he abruptly let go of her, sat upright, and shouted, "Who the hell wrote this crap, Steve?"

"Cut!" came the disgusted voice of the director, and the cameramen capped their lenses for the fifth time that scene.

In the control booth high above the block-long studio, Steve Bronsky rose from his seat behind the director, his fingers plowing angrily through his wavy dark hair. He looked down at the woman in the chair next to his, his brown eyes flaring. "Welcome to 'Search for Love,' Miss Arensen. This gives you an idea of what you're in for."

Cathy looked up at him, meeting his hostile glare with a poised half smile. "Ted Palmer is not exactly a team player, is he?"

"Team player? He's a self-centered fool. Doesn't have the sense to come in out of the rain...has an ego that runs larger than the national debt. Listen, when Ted hears a clap of thunder, he goes to the window and takes a bow."

She tapped her pen on the pad she was holding. "What kind of a contract is he on?" she asked calmly.

"Long-term, but we've always got that thirteeen-week option." He looked at her uneasily. "Thinking of dropping him?"

Cathy laid her pad and pen on the seat next to her and adjusted her horn-rimmed glasses. "'Search for Love' is in big trouble, Steve, or I wouldn't be here. According to the Nielsen ratings, it's in the pits as far as the soaps go. We don't have time to coddle a prima donna...there's too much work to be done." She saw him wince at her frankness.

"You come right to the point, don't you, Miss Arensen?"

"Anything else would be a waste of time, and"—she leaned back in her chair—"I wish you would call me Cathy. If we're going to work together, we owe it to the troops to give them the impression we're a team."

A wry smile crossed his mouth as he tugged at his right earlobe. "Will Catherine do?"

"No," she answered curtly.

"Very well, then...Cathy...shall we go down into the studio and see if we can calm Ted down?" He watched her get up; then his eyes assessed her, starting at her comfortable shoes and working their way up her tan business suit, fixing at last on the ash-blond hair pulled back into a bun. "Pity you're no sex goddess. Ted's rather susceptible to attractive women."

Cathy's hazel eyes narrowed, shooting sparks of green lightning at him; her clenched fists pulled down on the bottom of her tailored jacket. "If I were a sex goddess, Steve, I'd be working on the other side of the camera." Hiding the hurt that she felt tighten her chest, she stalked past him and started down the curved iron staircase to the studio below.

The bedroom set was at the far end of the soundstage, and as she walked past the other three-sided rooms that made up the various shooting areas for the daytime serial "Search for Love," or "SFL" as the cast and crew called it, she felt the actors rehearsing on the sets studying her as she passed them.

It was the end of her long first day on the show, and she knew they were all dubious about her being brought in as supervising producer, a title seemingly subordinate to Steve's executive producer, but carrying the power to make any changes she wanted, including cast, writers, or technical crew. Her one-year contract, she had made sure, gave her the powers she knew she would need if "SFL" were to make a turnaround and climb back up in the ratings. The only problem was that Steve Bronsky resented those powers.

She had been given the go-ahead by the network biggies largely because of her unqualified success with the popular California-based "Howardsville General" and "Days of our Loves'' daytime serials. At thirty-one, she had already earned the reputation of a no-nonsense, talented producer; one who could cope with the multifaceted problems that go into organizing a daily one-hour soap; one who could juggle 260 episodes a year filled with problems of casting, sets, music, technicians, and budget. And now, this was just what she needed—problems with the executive producer.

As Cathy reached the bedroom set, Vanessa, "SFL's" reigning villainess, was propping herself up against the bed's velvet headboard, looking irritated and bored. Ted Palmer sat on the edge of the bed, staring belligerently into space, nude from the waist up, appearing ridiculous in his jeans and red socks.

Just as Cathy was about to speak to him, Steve took hold of her arm from behind. "Let me handle this." Then, "Okay, Ted, what's the problem this time?"

Ted look up at him, his eyes wide with annoyance. "Steve, it's the stupid script. You heard it, didn't you...'I've dreamed about this a hundred times, but I never thought it would ever happen,'" he simpered. "What kind of garbage is that?"

Steve glanced sharply at Cathy and then back at Ted. "We're not doing Shakespeare, Ted. I realize that every word the writers give you may not thrill you to the core, but you're supposed to be an actor. I watched you on the monitor in the control booth. You looked and sounded like you were having gas pains."

Ted loomed up to his full six-three height, his handsome face scowling, his massive chest heaving. From his four-inch advantage over Steve, he glared at him. "Well just remember, ol' buddy, who it was that won the Emmy last year as the outstanding actor in a daytime drama series...before *you* lost interest in 'SFL.'"

An embarrassed hush swept over the set; Cathy saw the look of confusion and guilt settle on Steve's face. She stepped forward.

"You, Ted, are about to put yourself on the endangered-species list. You're holding up the taping and costing us time and money."

He glanced around at his cast mates, obviously not caring for a put-down from a woman. "Now listen, Miss Arensen, you're new here. You don't know what's been going—"

"No, Ted," she shot back, "*you* listen. Your contract doesn't give you script approval. Your job is to do your best to make whatever script you're given come alive, and that's where I want to see your efforts go. Is that clear?"

Chuckles from the cast and crew sent his hand brushing across his hairy chest nervously. "And *your* job, Miss Arensen, is to get some decent scripts from the so-called writers...not this slop we spend all night learning for the next day."

"Ted—" Steve started, but before he could continue, Cathy interrupted.

"I know exactly what my job is, Ted, and I'm going to see that it gets done."

Steve glanced at his watch. "Okay, people, it's after seven. It's been a long day. Let's wrap it up. Everyone get a rest this weekend and come in smiling Monday morning."

Cathy watched Ted storm off the set and head for the dressing rooms. "I see what you mean, Steve...about his ego. It's taller than he is."

"His fans sure love him, though. It's got to be his body, because he doesn't have much going for him between his ears."

They started back toward the staircase leading up to the control booth, but as they approached the set used for the show's nightclub scenes Cathy saw a tall young man dressed in a tux leaning against the bar.

He was staring at her brazenly with the most beautiful violet-blue eyes she had ever seen. Quickly, her mind previewed the many characters on "SFL" who had story lines, but his face matched none of them. She knew he was aware that she was studying him, studying the face that she could only describe as mysterious, fascinating.

"Steve," she asked suddenly, "who is that?"

He looked over at the young man leaning against the bar. "Him? I can't remember his name. He's new...just started this week...hired as an under-five player."

Cathy continued to study him as they neared the set. "No more than five speaking lines for someone who looks like that?" Her professional mind quickly assessed him to be about twenty-four, six feet tall, lean and muscular, wide at the shoulders, and extremely attractive in his short brown perm. "Steve, have them hold the lights and bring a camera over here."

"Now?"

"Please, Steve...now."

With a shrug, Steve went off to talk to the floor director, half watching Cathy as she walked up to the man on the set.

"Hello," she said, extending her hand, "I'm Cathy Arensen, supervising producer. I understand you're also new to 'SFL.'"

"Yes, I know who you are, Miss Arensen."

As he took her hand, Cathy had a feeling that he didn't smile easily, but she liked the voice she heard: it was low, musical, and it had a quality that was quite provocative; exciting, even. And the hand that held hers was strong and warm. Had she not withdrawn it herself, she felt he would gladly have held it longer.

"Sorry we didn't get to tape your scene today," she apologized. "Do you have experience on other daytime dramas...uh...I'm sorry, I don't even know your name." Again she caught herself apologizing.

"Devlin...Devlin Howard."

"Devlin," she repeated. "Nice. What name are the writers using for you?"

He leaned backward again, resting his elbows on the bar, his gorgeous blue eyes focusing clearly and intimately on her. "Jake Carter."

Cathy could tell that he wasn't thrilled with his character's name. "You don't look like a Jake to me." She wished he would blink or something, but he didn't. "Would you prefer Devlin Carter?"

She watched as the silver flecks appeared in his eyes, as the corners of his beautiful mouth insinuated a smile.

"Devlin Carter," he repeated slowly. "Yes, I like the sound of that much better."

"Here we are," Steve said, not bothering to hide the annoyance in his voice as he preceded the cameraman rolling the heavy camera toward the set.

"Devlin, just stay where you are for a minute," Cathy directed. Then, "No, just left a little. Get that key light on your face." She moved toward the cameraman. "Let me see a tight head shot." He racked his lens, focused, and then stepped aside so Cathy could check out the shot.

"Steve," she called, and he joined her in back of the camera. "Look."

He looked in the viewfinder. "So?" he asked dryly.

"The eyes...look at those eyes." She moved to the side of the camera. "Devlin, look camera right."

Automatically the cameraman moved in and framed Devlin's close-up profile and refocused. Again, Cathy checked the viewfinder, motioning Steve to take a look.

"Now camera left, Devlin," she ordered.

As she and Steve checked out the shot, Cathy quietly said, "He doesn't even have a bad side...and those eyes!"

Steve straightened up and leaned against the huge camera. "What's with you, Arensen...an eye fetish?"

Cathy looked at him icily and decided not to answer. "Did you see his audition?"

"Of course I did. Why?"

"Don't you think he can handle a story line?"

"Listen, Cathy, he came in as an extra, and I'm the one that suggested him for an under-five. And now, you see those blue eyes and you want to make him a star!"

Knowing that Devlin could hear them, she turned her back to the set and lowered her voice. "Calm down, Steve. I just think he's got potential, and don't forget we need all the help we can get if we're going to resurface in the charts."

He looked at her warily and then over at Devlin. "And you think blue eyes is going to do it for us?"

"Not alone." She glanced over toward the bedroom set and saw that Vanessa was still there, watching them with great interest. "I've got an idea, Steve. Keep the camera open."

With that, she walked toward the bedroom set as Vanessa began arranging her blouse.

Vanessa Rockwell. For years she'd been the number one vixen on "SFL," Cathy reflected. She was thirty-four, but she looked twenty-five. On camera she was statuesque, a green-eyed beauty with luxuriant auburn hair, dyed to perfection.

"Working late, Miss Arensen?" Vanessa asked cheerfully.

"Aren't we all. Vanessa, I've a favor to ask you."

"Sure," she said agreeably.

"Would you mind running through a quick scene with Devlin? I want to see how he'll handle it."

Vanessa's green eyes lit up. If anything, she loved doing bedroom scenes, and she hadn't missed Devlin in the studio the past week. "Well, you just get him right over here, then, Miss Arensen."

"Cathy...please."

"Okay, Cathy. I'll do my best to get him in the mood."

Cathy's voice echoed across the almost empty studio as she called the three men to the bedroom set.

"What are you up to now?" Steve asked, looking at his watch.

"This will only take a minute, Steve. I want to see Devlin go through Ted's scene with Vanessa."

"Ted's scene?" he asked quizzically, eyeing the smiling young man Cathy was rushing to the bed on the set.

"Get your jacket and shirt off, Devlin, and hop in next to Vanessa. Did you hear this scene earlier with Ted?"

"No," he told her as he stripped to the waist, exposing his well-formed body, "we were blocking on our set."

Cathy looked at Vanessa. "What was that line Ted was complaining about?"

Before she could answer, Steve chimed in. "I've dreamed about this a hundred times, but I never thought it would happen."

"Got that, Devlin?" she asked, laying his shirt and coat on the bottom of the bed.

Nodding his head curtly, Devlin took off his shoes and then slipped under the satin sheet. As he was about to put his arm around Vanessa, she told him to wait a moment. Slipping under the protection of the sheet, she removed her blouse.

"The more realistic, the better, I always say," she murmured sweetly as she cuddled close to Devlin's solid chest, brushing her slender, well-manicured fingers over his shoulders.

Cathy was suddenly embarrassed to find Devlin's eyes set upon hers, knowing that he saw the look of disapproval on her face when Vanessa removed her blouse. She felt even more uncomfortable when the corner of his mouth lifted in a knowing smile. Quickly, she instructed the cameraman. "Give me a tight two-shot, please." He set it up and focused. "A little tighter," she requested. "Yes, that's great. Okay, Devlin...now."

Devlin held Vanessa for a moment, saying nothing. Then he brushed back the hair that curved over her forehead and tenderly kissed her brow. When he did speak, his voice oozed warmth and sexuality. "I've dreamed about this a hundred times...no, not a hundred...a thousand," he ad-libbed, taking his time, kissing her hair, "but I never thought it would really happen." His voice trailed off as he leaned over her, at first only brushing her lips with his, but then his mouth began a slow, sensual grind on hers.

"Enough already!" Steve said loudly.

Cathy was still looking through the camera's viewfinder as Devlin moved off of Vanessa, his face businesslike and questioning. But it was Vanessa's face that startled her. Vanessa was an experienced actress on daytime soaps and had done many a torrid bed scene, but now the look on her face was one of surprise—and delight, and that was exactly the reaction Cathy wanted from "SFL's" viewers.

She moved from behind the camera. "That was good, Devlin, very good."

"And now can we all go home?" Steve asked with mock politeness.

"Yes, of course," she answered somewhat absently, watching Devlin get up from the bed. "I'm sorry to have kept you all so late."

"Any time, Miss Arensen," Vanessa chirped. "I mean. . .Cathy." Still smiling, she leaned back on her elbows and watched Devlin pick up his shirt from the bottom of the bed. "It's a helluva job, but somebody's got to do it."

Steve lifted Vanessa's chin good-naturedly. "You're all heart, lady." Then, seeing Cathy still watching Devlin as he buttoned his shirt, Steve picked up Devlin's jacket and tossed it to him. "See me Monday, Devlin. We'll talk new contract."

Still, Devlin said nothing, but his eyes sent a smile of thanks to the new supervising producer, an intimate smile that caused Cathy to smile back.

As she started to leave the studio, Steve caught her arm. "Got time for a quick one?"

The pleasantness of his voice surprised her; it was different from the businesslike tone he had used during their long day at work, which was spent watching tapes, going over upcoming scripts, analyzing the long-term story projections for the show's fourteen actors with story lines, meeting with writers, and spot-checking selected mail from "SFL's" television audience.

"Thanks, Steve, but I'm exhausted. I haven't even unpacked yet. I slept on the plane from California and all I had time for this morning was a quick shower and a cup of coffee."

He opened the door to the control booth for her and she collected her things. "Have you found a place already?"

"No...staying with friends," she told him as she sank into a chair facing a wall of blank TV monitors. She hoped she didn't look as tired as she felt.

For a moment he studied her face, and for the first time he realized that she had been going full steam all day long and was about to run out of fuel—and he also realized that he admired her abilities, that she really did know what she was doing. A regret began to gnaw at him, a regret that his welcome had been so cold, a regret that his own problems had overriden his usual good-naturedness.

"Listen, Cathy, we're closed down this weekend. You've got two days to catch up on your sleep. One drink won't hurt."

She looked over at him as he slouched against the railing behind the director's console. Again he surprised her. The brown eyes that had only glared at her previously were now smiling warmly. The control booth was in semidarkness, with only the dim night lights breaking the eerie stillness of the usually busy director's lair. The soft light spread across

Steve's rugged face, across his attractive mouth and pleasantly full lips; and in the brief moment she searched his face, she noticed the small scar at his right temple.

"One drink?" he repeated, bringing a soft smile to her face.

"One drink," she agreed.

From their window seat in the Rainbow Room on the sixty-fifth floor of the RCA building, Cathy looked out over sparkling mid-town Manhattan. Hollywood's skyline, in comparison, was as flat as a cornfield.

She was relieved when the music settled into rhythm-and-blues, music that was more relaxing—and that was what she wanted to do, just relax. All day long she had presented the image of a fairly hardened businesswoman, one who was confident, totally capable, on top of it all, but now she was dragging and she knew she couldn't retreat to the quiet, pleasant apartment she had in Hollywood.

Although she loved the dear friends who had invited her to stay with them in their West Side apartment until she found a place of her own, she knew that when she returned there that evening she would still be keyed up. Relax, that was what she wanted to do most right now, and maybe the Rob Roy she was holding would help.

"Welcome to New York, Cathy."

His voice brought her back from her momentary reverie, and she realized that she was actually in New York with a mammoth job ahead of her, and she was thankful that the man across from her, a man with whom she would be working very closely, was being friendlier than he had been all day.

She sipped her drink. "Thanks, Steve, but I'm not sure coming here was the smartest move I've ever made."

His smile vanished. "Why do you say that?"

"You'd laugh if I told you." She took off her glasses and searched her handbag for their case. "In fact, I'm about to laugh myself."

"Try me."

She looked up at him, and for the first time he saw her eyes clearly—lovely hazel eyes touched by a delicate green glow. Without her glasses, her whole face softened; even her voice seemed more mellow to him.

"I'm a grown woman, Steve, and I'm homesick. Right now I wish I were back in California."

"What's age got to do with being homesick? I leave New York for a vacation and I get homesick...can't wait till I get back."

Again she sipped her drink. "Are you one of those natives who are supercilious toward those unfortunate enough not to be New Yorkers?" she asked, smiling.

"Well, Miss Hollywood, after all Manhattan's the most fabulous island in the recorded history of man. Where else can you travel three or four miles and feel like you've been on a trip around the world?"

She glanced out the window again and gazed at the huge skyscrapers that lit up the dark night. "Maybe it's the size of the buildings that frightens me. Their giantism seems to parallel the job we've got ahead of us: the resuscitation of 'SFL.'"

From the look on his face, Cathy knew she had hit a nerve, and silently she berated herself for having brought up the fact that an outsider had to be imported to help Steve Bronsky, executive producer of the once most popular daytime drama on television. But now that she had broached the matter, she decided to venture on.

"Steve, what did happen? Why did the show take such a nosedive in the ratings this past year?"

His head shot up and again she saw the hard look of the man she had spent the day with. "Don't push me on that, Cathy. Not now."

Tired and irritated by his brusqueness, she finished her drink quickly, too quickly, and reached for her handbag. Knowing she was about to leave him sitting there, he grabbed her wrist with such force that she dropped her bag.

"My, but you're a sensitive young lady."

"I'm not that young," she snapped back at him, "and let go of me."

"All right...you're a sensitive old lady."

Hating the soft smile she saw on his face, she glared at him. "Look, we've had our one drink and that's all I want from you. That's all I'll ever want from you."

Still he held on to her. "You're so smug, Miss Arensen, so sure of yourself, the big deal they've flown in from the West Coast to make 'SFL' rise from the ashes. Well, listen and listen good. You can't do it all alone. You're going to need me right along beside you to pull that one off."

Oblivious to the people watching them, she pulled her hand free from his grasp, snatched her handbag up, and stood beside the small table. "Don't flatter yourself, Steve Bronsky. I don't need you or anyone else." With that, she made a beeline for the elevator.

Steve quickly tossed a few bills on the table and caught up with her, but not before seeing her place one hand against the wall near the elevator door as though for support.

The door opened and she rushed inside. He followed. "Are you okay?" he asked, seeing that her tanned face looked pale.

Cathy shrugged off the hand that held her arm. "Yes, I'm okay. I haven't eaten since last night...in California to be exact. I guess that Rob Roy hit me."

"No breakfast and no lunch. That was clever."

Suddenly the elevator shot down from the sixty-fifth floor and Cathy thought her stomach had relocated somewhere near her throat. "Dear God," she moaned, "now I know what a reentry from space must be like."

Once outside the building, the hot August air hit her like a thick wall. Again she slumped, and Steve took hold of her arm.

"C'mon. You need something to eat," he said, leading her to Fifth Avenue, where he hailed a cab.

Cathy hadn't the strength to object. She had wanted to relax, and that one drink on her empty stomach was forcing her to do just that.

"Where to?" the blond-haired young cabbie asked.

"The Village...St. Luke's and Seventh," Steve directed, watching Cathy as she leaned back against the seat and closed her eyes.

The woman who had appeared to be so much in control during that day at the studio, who had seemed to be on top of everything, now looked to him to be rather helpless, and suddenly he was overwhelmed with a desire to protect her.

He directed the cabbie to pull up in front of a tree-shaded four-story town house behind high front steps lined with wrought-iron railings.

Cathy let herself be led past the soft light of the lamppost at the bottom of the stone steps, and then down several steps under the main stairway toward a mahogany door fitted with shiny brass. Inside, she heard the door close behind her.

"This isn't a restaurant," she said quickly.

Taking her arm, Steve walked her through the foyer and into his living room, which was long and high-ceilinged, pleasantly comfortable with its pale green carpet, over-sized pearl gray sofa, and matching easy chairs. Pale yellow floor-to-ceiling draperies reflected in the huge mirror that hung over the white Italian marble fireplace.

"If I thought you could have sat up long enough, I would have taken you to a restaurant, but you look like you're going to collapse on me any minute." He took her handbag from her and tossed it on one of the easy chairs. "Give me your jacket and make yourself comfortable while I rustle up something to eat."

Before she could object she felt his hands slipping the jacket from her shoulders. "Now wait just a minute. I didn't say I was staying."

"Don't be ridiculous. I am *not* Jack the Ripper. All I'm going to do is feed you."

Cathy's jacket fell on top of her handbag and then he shrugged out of his suit coat and went into the kitchen, returning with a glass of cold milk.

"Here, drink this."

"I hate milk," she complained.

"Drink it. It'll put the bloom back in that tan of yours."

Dubiously, she took the glass and, seeing that he was watching her, sipped some, thinking he would go away if she did. But he didn't. He just stood there waiting for her to drink more.

"I'm drinking, I'm drinking!" she cried, taking a gulp to satisfy him; but as soon as he returned to the kitchen she put the glass down on the marble-topped table next to the sofa and leaned back against the comfortable softness of the cushions, feeling as if her stomach were about to argue with the cold milk.

Suddenly he was there again, looking at her and then at the almost full glass of milk. Automatically she reached for the glass, cursing it under her breath.

"That's my good little girl," he said condescendingly.

"I'm not your little girl," she fired back at him, "and what's with you and milk? Do you own a dairy or something?"

He leaned down and patted her cheek lightly. "Now, now, I understand. Hunger makes me testy, too."

Roughly she brushed his fingers away from her face, making a childish grimace in response to the wide smile on his, and then she watched him walk across the room to the wall unit, his steps long and graceful, his fitted shirt outlining his wide shoulders and powerful back muscles.

As he placed a cassette into the stereo, her eyes went from his strong-looking back to the football trophy on the mantel of the fireplace—then back to him as she heard the soothing orchestral strings well into the lush adagio of Rachmanioff's Second Symphony.

Turning toward her, he smiled, pulled his tie off, unbuttoned the top buttons of his dress shirt, and rolled its cuffs almost up to his elbows. Yes, she thought, he had the arms to be an ex-football player.

"Comfortable?" he asked quietly.

Suddenly, Cathy felt all her annoyances slip away. Perhaps it was the relaxing music; perhaps it was because he was being a perfect gentleman and extremely considerate. Whatever the reason, she felt her body begin to unwind.

"Yes, I'm quite comfortable." Then, softly, she murmured, "Thanks."

Walking back toward the kitchen, he said, "Just be another minute"—he stopped and turned—"and...drink your milk."

The seriousness with which he said it made her chuckle quietly, but then she began to laugh and the laughter poured out until her eyes teared and she all but doubled up. The shocked look on Steve's face made her laugh even more.

"You okay?"

His look of deep concern only fueled her wild, uncontrollable laughter. Her whole body shook until her breathing became erratic. Steve sat next to her and began slapping her back.

Coughing, she choked out, "Okay...I'm okay. Just stop beating on me!"

"What's so funny?" His confusion was obvious in his tone.

"This damn milk." Still giggling, she wiped away her tears with the handkerchief he gave her. "Right now this milk seems to be the most important thing in the whole world to both of us."

Steve leaned back, relieved, letting his hands rest in his lap. "You're a kook, did you know that? A real kook."

She looked at him as he sat next to her, examining her face. He was serious, she could see it in his eyes. *He thinks I'm a kook,* she told herself, and then the deep chuckles started again.

Steve stood up abruptly. "I'd better get you something to eat. You're getting hysterical."

Only after he had left the room was she able to calm down. He was right, she thought, she was becoming hysterical. She took several deep breaths, and as she settled down she realized that every muscle in her body ached from the painful laughter. She hadn't been able to control it. A quick self-analysis told her that the whole day had been a mess of tension for her. The late-night flight from California, the not eating, the new high-powered job, new faces, no place to call her own in which to curl up and refresh frayed nerves—all of it had suddenly burst out in her crazy laughter.

Exhausted, Cathy lay back, letting her tired body nestle in the softness of the sofa. With the strains of Rachmaninoff flowing about her, her eyelids closed, and in a moment she was asleep.

Chapter Two

Cathy felt comfortable as she shifted her head deeper into the softness of the pillow under it. Slowly her lashes opened a fraction as she inhaled an unfamiliar fragrance, a clean-smelling lime aroma that drifted from the pillow into her nostrils. She liked it, and as she inhaled deeper, she wriggled her toes, realizing she still had her stockings on. Reaching up to scratch her shoulder, the silky feel of her blouse caused her eyes to snap open. She shot up to a sitting position and tried to get her bearings. The sofa, the fireplace; and sitting across from her in an easy chair, she saw Steve watching her intently, sending her a warm smile from across the room.

"Feel better?" he asked softly.

Cathy ran her fingers roughly through her hair, causing the disheveled bun to break free, allowing her hair to fall loosely around her shoulders. Automatically she fluffed it to give it some sense of order.

"What?" Her brain worked feverishly until she organized her thoughts. "I guess I dozed off. I'm sorry, Steve." She threw back the comforter he had placed over her and looked for the shoes he had obviously removed from her feet.

"Sorry for what? You were exhausted...you needed that little nap."

"What time is it?" Even as she asked, she looked at her wristwatch. "Dear God, it's after midnight. Why didn't you wake me? Helen and Fred will think I've been mugged." She jumped up from the sofa, trying to decide just what to do next.

"Cathy, why don't you phone them, let them know you're all right, and tell them you're staying here for the night?"

Now she was wide awake. "Staying here? Don't be ridiculous."

"What's so ridiculous about it? Going clear uptown in the middle of the night and keeping your friends up until you get there, that's ridiculous." Tugging at his earlobe, he said, "Besides, you haven't eaten yet."

"Please, Steve, don't start that again."

Leaning back in his chair, he brought one leg up and rested its ankle on his other knee. "What's the matter? Are you afraid to spend the night here?" Even in the dimly lighted room his brown eyes shone brightly.

"Afraid? Of course not. Don't be silly," she said as she tucked her blouse inside her belted skirt.

"I think you are," he said smugly.

"Read my lips, Steve. I said I am *not* afraid. Fear has nothing to do with it."

He lit a cigarette and blew the smoke out in a smooth, relaxed stream. "Then what's the problem?"

"What's the problem?" she repeated. Then, after thinking a moment, she said, "The problem is that I don't feel right landing on your doorstep like a waif in need of somewhere to sleep."

"There are three bedrooms upstairs on the second floor. I'll even arrange it so there's an empty room between us."

Eyeing him suspiciously, she asked, "You live here alone?"

"All alone. The first two floors are mine, and I rent the top two out, so it's not as though we'll be alone in the house."

It worried her that he was beginning to make sense, and it would take only a minute to call Helen. And he was right, her friends would feel obligated to wait up for her if she did try to get back to their apartment.

"You're sure I wouldn't be a problem...that is, if I decide to stay." Her tone was hesitant, but already she knew she had decided.

Steve's right hand raised in an oath. "No problem...honest. The phone's in the next room on the desk. Now go call them."

As Cathy reached for her bag to get her address book, Steve switched on the light in his study and began to try to make some kind of order from the piles of papers and folders strewn carelessly on his desk.

"You're not too well organized, are you?" she commented, surveying the mess on top of his desk.

She saw his jaw stiffen.

"That, my dear, is exactly why the big boys seduced you into coming over here from the West Coast. To organize me, to patch me up...make me whole again." With that, he turned abruptly and left her alone to make her call.

For a moment Cathy reflected on what her host had just said—to patch him up, to make him whole again. She didn't pretend to understand what he had meant by that, but she did know that for years he had successfully run the "SFL" ship upstream in the ratings and that for some reason he had recently lost control in the stormy sea of daytime competition.

Quickly she made her call, giving Helen Steve's phone number, apologizing and half explaining why she wouldn't return that night, assuring her that she was in good hands.

"In good hands," she repeated as she put the receiver down. Then she thought to herself, how could she possibly be sure of that? What did she really know about Steven Bronsky? He had behaved well—so far. And then she recalled his having pointed out that she was no sex goddess. Well, that was all right with her, she told herself solidly. She didn't want to be a sex goddess. She wanted her career and the uncomplicated life she now led, and no man was going to change that.

"Come and get it!"

"Coming," she answered, switching off the light in the study.

"It ain't much," he apologized, "but what do you expect from a bachelor's refrigerator?"

Cathy looked down at the tray he had set on the table between the two easy chairs. This had definitely not been her day, she told herself as she forced a hint of a smile, looking down at the bagels, cream cheese, and lox he had fixed. At least there was no milk in sight, and the coffee did smell good.

"Dig in," he ordered, tossing a huge napkin over her lap and then taking one of the thickly stuffed bagels for himself.

After another look at the lox she said, "Steve...maybe just some coffee."

"Why? Don't you like bagels and lox?"

"Not really in the middle of the night, I don't."

He pulled a little piece of lox from her bagel. "Open," he ordered. "Lox is good for you any time of day...or night."

He held the fish to her lips and Cathy could feel her nostrils flare at the salty smell of it. Gingerly she opened her mouth and let him place the lox inside, hating the smile of satisfaction he showed as she began to chew slowly—very slowly.

Quickly she washed it down with a mouthful of coffee and then took heart, picked up the bagel, and took a bite. "Steve," she asked after finally swallowing her first mouthful, "when did this bagel first see the light of day?"

While chewing, he mumbled, "They're supposed to be firm."

"I know, but firm is firm and tough is tough."

After more coffee, Cathy was pleasantly surprised to find that her stomach had no plans to reject the midnight meal; in fact, it seemed to welcome the long-overdue sustenance.

"That should make you feel better," he said, sincerely concerned.

Glancing over at his attractive face, Cathy took note of the little dab of cream cheese that stuck to the corner of his mouth. Then her eyes seemed to be much too interested in the sensual fullness of his lips as she watched the rhythmic motion of his strong jawline while he enthusiastically devoured his second bagel.

"You do feet better, don't you?"

Startled by the sound of his voice, she forced her eyes away from his when she realized he knew she had been staring at him. "Uh...yes, I do. This is delicious."

And now she knew he was staring at her, and try as she might, she could not make eating her bagel and lox a delicate maneuver. A furtive glance toward him told her he was still watching, and it was making her nervous. So, she decided, she would make conversation.

"How'd you get that scar, Steve...football?"

His fingers swept across the slender two-inch scar, which began at the hairline at his right temple. "You psychic or something?"

"Hardly." His eyes followed hers over to the trophy on the mantel. "Just observant."

Finished with his sandwich Steve lit a cigarette. "A souvenir from my college days. Picture this." With cigarette tucked onto ashtray edge, he stood up. "A bulletlike forward pass coming at me." He turned his head, looking angularly at the imaginary ball. "It's thrown high. I leap gracefully into the air and pluck the pigskin from space." With arms stretched, pantomiming his daring feat, he continued, "A one-handed catch of the fourteen-yarder"—he grunted—"and then I land with the finesse of Baryshnikov. The crowd roars and my feet become a blur as I lunge between would-be tacklers toward the goal line, but then I make a *big* mistake."

Holding the imaginary leather, he looked behind him. "I glance over my shoulder to see how far I've left the bruisers behind...only to find out they're pulling in the breath

I'm exhaling. When they peeled those suckers off me, Gorilla George's foot was half-way up my safety helmet.'' Again he traced his scar. ''Well, at least his foot was safe. And that, Cathy Arensen, was when I decided I had had enough football.''

The easy chair was wide enough for Cathy to curl up in, so as Steve finished his heroic tale, she pushed off her shoes and angled her legs on the soft chair.

''How'd you land in TV?'' she asked.

''Communications major.''

He poured more coffee for the two of them and then picked up the tray and started for the kitchen, talking louder as the distance widened between them.

''After a stint in Vietnam as a cryptographer, I landed a job as technical director in TV sports, but seeing that was a financial dead end, I decided to get into production. I thought soaps would be a stepping-stone to prime time, but once involved I became fascinated with this business of love.'' As he appeared in the doorway from the kitchen, he leaned against it and smiled enigmatically. ''This business of make-believe love, I mean.''

Cathy had rested her head against the high back of the easy chair, enjoying the way he walked gracefully to and from the kitchen, liking the mellow sound of his rich baritone voice as he gave her a cursory glimpse into his life. Much to her surprise she wanted to know more about him.

He stopped in front of her chair, his large hands dug into his hips. ''Is the story of my fascinating life about to put you to sleep?''

''No.'' She smiled. ''I'm just feeling very relaxed.''

Hooking his finger through the two handles of their coffee mugs, he said, ''C'mon, let's get some fresh air.''

Cathy slipped into her shoes and followed him through the French doors out onto a small deck in the walled garden behind the house. To the left, under a wooden overhang, she saw a sunken Jacuzzi, privacy assured by the luxuriant vines that threaded up the latticework supporting the overhang. To the right, there were two pillowed lounge chairs and a small white table.

"Lean back and enjoy," he said quietly, easing himself out to his full length in one chair. "And take your shoes off."

"I will if you will," she said, and watched him kick his off.

Settled back in her chair, Cathy looked up at the sky. The night was clear, somewhat humid, but the stars glowed in the dark sky. The soft sound of an oboe mingled with distant traffic noises. Perhaps she imagined it, but she thought the air was slightly salt-laden, and then she remembered that Manhattan was a little island, an island held in the grip of an ocean and rivers.

Suddenly she was overwhelmed by a feeling of peace and contentment, a feeling that everything was right. For some unfathomable reason she experimented—imagining that Steve was not lying close to her on the little deck, and in that instant she lost the feeling of peace and contentment.

Almost sensing her distress, Steve angled a look at her. "What are you thinking about so hard?"

"Oh, just that I like your hideaway. Is it always this peaceful out here?"

Stretching his arms overhead, he then placed his palms in back of his head. "In the middle of the night it is." He paused. Then he asked, "Do you really like it?"

"I just said I did," she answered wryly.

Now he looked up at the stars. "Why don't you move in with me?"

Cathy bolted upright, almost knocking over the little table as she did so. "Move in with you?"

Still he didn't look at her. "You said you liked it."

"What's that got to do with it? I like the Taj Mahal, but I'm not about to move in there."

"You don't have a place of your own," he reminded her.

"So, I'll get one."

"Do you plan to stay in New York after your one-year contract is up?"

"No, I'm going to make a beeline back to California. I told you—I'm homesick already."

Steve raised himself up, resting on his elbows, and now he looked at her. "Seems like a lot of trouble to try to find a decent apartment that's going to cost you your eyeteeth for only a few months."

"For twelve months," she said nervously.

"Okay, twelve months." He lay back down on the lounge, looking at the starry sky. "Seriously though, Cathy, you and I are going to be working very closely together. You know what the days at the studio are going to be like. We won't have time to do any real planning. It'll be a matter of putting fires out all day long. That means after-hours meetings, weekend sessions. One of us taking a cab to meet the other. And I've got the room here. You'd even have your own bathroom."

Cathy reached for her coffee mug and took a swallow. It was cold, but she needed to do something to make her stop thinking that he was making a great deal of sense.

Without raising himself, he looked over at her. "What do you say, C.A.? Wanna be buddies?"

She looked at him lying there, the whites of his eyes making the warm brown of his pupils look like puppy dog eyes, the short, wavy dark hair making him look more like a gladiator than an executive producer. Damn, she thought, he was becoming more attractive by the minute, and she didn't like the feelings that were surging through her. It would be so easy to say yes and to— "No, Steve, no way, but thanks for the offer." She bit her lips but was glad she had said what she did. "May I have one of your cigarettes, please?"

"Cigarette? I didn't think you smoked." He took the pack from his shirt pocket.

"I quit about a year ago, but I feel the urge now."

Back went the cigarettes into his pocket. "Then you don't need to start again." He got up and went inside, returning with a small dish of mints. "Here, suck on one of these." She took one and he went on, "Cathy. Surely you've seen 'Three's Company' on TV."

She nodded.

"Look how well they get along with no hanky-panky. Why couldn't we do the same?"

She took the mint from her mouth and held it between two fingers. "With three you have a referee...and a witness." She popped the mint back in her mouth.

"Don't you trust me?"

After swallowing what remained of the mint, she said, "I trust you."

He sat up and rested his arms on his knees, clasping his hands together. A half smile formed on his lips. "Don't you trust yourself?"

Now she was furious. She stood up and was about to lash out at him. Instead she turned away and sauntered back into the living room.

Steve followed and closed the door behind him. He turned to her and raised one hand. "Whoa. What did I say that upset you? I only meant to point out that if you trusted me and you trusted yourself, how could we ever have a problem living under the same roof for a few months?"

Cathy stopped pacing, crossed her arms, and forced a smile. "That's a naïve point of view for a man of your intelligence and experience, Steve."

"Intelligent, yes. Experienced...I guess so."

"What would your lady friends think about my living here with you?"

"Nothing," he said quickly.

"Nothing?" That surprised her. "Well...what about your reputation?"

Steve sat down on the sofa, stretched his legs, and slid his hands into his pockets. "I'm a man, Cathy. I don't have to worry about my reputation."

"Then what about mine?" she blurted out.

"You're going back to California. What difference will it make a year from now? And look how convenient it will be for both of us."

Too convenient, she thought to herself.

"Don't decide now, Cathy. Sleep on it and we'll talk about it again in the morning. Okay?"

"Morning? It's almost morning now. What time is it?"

"A little after two," he said casually.

"Sleep...that's what I need more than anything else in the world right now," she murmured.

The ceilings upstairs were not as high as the ones on the first floor, but the bedroom Steve led Cathy to was large and airy. It had obviously been a woman's bedroom at one time: the long vanity and the pale yellow decor had a woman's touch about it.

"I think you'll be comfortable in here. The bathroom's right in there." He pointed to the other side of the room as he walked to the hallway door. "I'll be right back."

When he disappeared down the hallway, Cathy eyed the bed. The covers had been pulled back carefully. Had he done that while she was asleep, assuming that she would agree to spend the night? she wondered. Of course he had, she decided.

He whistled as he reentered the room carrying towels and a small plastic package. Tossing the towels onto the bed, he tore into the package and withdrew a new pair of white pajamas.

"This will have to do, I'm afraid." He held the top up against her. "A Christmas present, but I never use pajamas."

"Well, I certainly hope you don't walk in your sleep."

He smiled. "It would be a first if I should. I'll get you a toothbrush and some toothpaste. There's soap in there already."

Again he left, taking his usual long, graceful strides, whistling happily.

Cathy's room was at the back of the house; from her window she could look down into the small garden below and into the gardens on either side. Even in the darkness she could tell that they were neatly kept and charming little sanctuaries for the occupants of the adjoining houses. Angling her head, she looked directly down at the redwood deck in back of the house, noticing that the wooden overhang did indeed give the hot tub a certain privacy.

"Here you go." He handed her a new toothbrush and tube of toothpaste. "I think that's about everything you'll need tonight."

"This morning, you mean," she countered.

"This morning...right. Listen, I'm sorry if I kept you up all night."

"I'm the one who's sorry, Steve. I know you didn't plan on nursing a weary newcomer to the Big Apple. You must have had other plans for the evening."

"It was a nice evening, Cathy, very nice." Taking her hand, he squeezed it gently. "Get a good night's sleep now. You look like you could use it." He stopped at the doorway. "Oh, leave your door open. The circulation will be better." Then, seeing the look of concern cloud her face, he explained, "I'm at the other end of the hallway, and I don't walk in my sleep." He smiled that charming smile of his. "Honest." And then he was gone from her view.

Cathy closed the door and slipped into the pajamas he had left her. Wearing the bottoms would be ridiculous; the top was as long as her summer nightie, although twice as wide. Quickly she washed her face and headed straight for the big, comfortable bed.

Just as she was about to slip under the pale green sheet, she stopped, thought a moment, and then opened the door to her room. In the darkness of the hallway she could see a weak shaft of light that she assumed came from Steve's room. Then she crawled into bed and let her head fall back on the soft pillow.

A deep sigh rushed from her throat and all the tension of the day seemed to flow out with it. She was exhausted, but not so relaxed that she could drift off immediately. She turned over on her stomach—the way she always fell asleep. Through half-closed eyes she saw the shaft of light in the hallway disappear. Her sluggish consciousness pictured Steve approaching his bed and settling down to a night's rest; pictured him, as he said, sans pajamas.

Her fingertips began a slow design on her pillow as she thought of the man called Steven Bronsky: ex-football player, ex-army man, likes classical music and bagels and lox and milk—ex-sports director and now executive producer of ''Search for Love.'' ''What a combination,'' she mumbled into her pillow. Her eyelids became heavier and heavier as her thinking became more disjointed. *Move in with him? Not on your life, Catherine. "Three's Company"...such an athletic body...that smile...every night...just down the hall...doesn't even wear pajamas...such a nice guy...so—*

Cathy's breathing deepened and every muscle in her body relaxed as her consciousness darkened, but before complete blackness overtook her, she imagined the ruggedly handsome lines of Steve's smiling face near hers, his strong arm over her body, drawing her closer to him as he lay beside her. And then, in her sleep, her lips quivered ever so lightly as they touched the warmth of his.

Chapter Three

Waffles and syrup, scrambled eggs and sausage, buttered English muffins and hot steaming coffee: these were the lovely dream aromas that invaded Cathy's nostrils just before waking. But as she slowly opened her heavy eyelids only the smell of coffee lingered.

Through strands of wayward hair she forced her lids open to discover that the yellow draperies of the window had been closed over the sheer panels, subduing the light of the day from outside. The unfamiliar surroundings brought her to full consciousness, and as she rolled over, brushing the hair away from her eyes, her thoughts went through an instant replay of the previous evening with Steve.

At the soft knock on the open door of the bedroom she bolted upright.

"Rested?" he asked softly.

The warmth in his voice filled her ears; his smiling eyes inspected her. Leaning back on one elbow, she looked at him standing there as though waiting for permission to come closer, his short-sleeved sport shirt snugly outlining his muscular physique.

Cathy raked her fingers through her loose tresses, trying to improve what she knew must be a tangled mess. "I feel great, as though I've slept for a day. What time is it?"

"Almost four."

"In the afternoon! Why didn't you wake me?"

She started to throw back the covers, but quickly recovered herself, remembering she had foregone the use of his pajama bottoms.

"You needed the sleep. What's the big deal—it's Saturday." He invited himself in and sat at the bottom of the bed.

"Oh, Helen's probably going crazy," she moaned, wishing he would leave so she could get dressed and phone her friend.

"No she isn't," he said casually.

Cathy stared at him. That innocent smile worried her. She had already started to recognize his various tones of voice—and the one he had just used alerted her.

"And why won't she be worried?"

He reached over and tickled the end of her nose. "Because she called early this morning, checking up on you."

"Oh. . .well, do you mind if I shower before I leave, Steve?"

"Leave? Why?" He feigned surprise at the idea.

"Why? Good Lord, do you think I'm going to live in the clothes I wore all day yesterday? I've got to get to Helen's and unpack, and I've got a lot of thinking to do about 'SFL' this weekend.''

He corrected her. ''*We* have a lot of thinking to do about 'SFL' this weekend.''

''I still have to unpack, Steve.''

''Okay.''

He got up and went to the hallway. When he returned carrying her suitcases and dress bag, Cathy's eyes widened.

''My luggage! How...what is it doing here? How did you—''

''When Helen phoned this morning, I simply told her you were sleeping and that I was renting you an apartment...that you'd be staying here. A quick cab trip to her place, and''—after hanging her dress bag in the closet, he turned—''you know, Cathy, that Helen is really a nice lady. She likes you a lot. And she thinks I'll be good for you.''

Cathy eyed her suitcases in disbelief, and when her sputtering stopped she exploded. ''You *what*? You decided that I would live with you? How dare you?'' She was half out of bed this time before she quickly retreated behind the sheet. ''Get out of here. Now! And don't think for a minute that you're going to get away with this, Steve. I know exactly what you're up to.''

''Calm down, C.A.'' He placed her makeup case on the vanity. ''I was just trying to be considerate. I thought we had agreed you'd be staying.''

''We agreed nothing of the kind. All you want is a live-in playmate!''

''Is that what you really think?'' A seriousness covered his words and his look. ''Well, if you want us to be playmates, I think I can handle that.''

"That's *not* what I meant, and you know it! Now, will you please get out of here so I can get up?"

"Fine, I will." He started out the door, but just as she jumped up from the bed he stuck his head back in the doorway. His eyes scanned her bare legs, which looked long and shapely. "There's a hair dryer in the cabinet in case you don't have one."

The pillow she threw missed him and landed in the hallway. Again his head appeared, his face one big gorgeous smile. "Would you like me to bring you up some coffee to have while you do whatever it is you do in there?" He caught the next pillow. "I guess not," he said matter-of-factly. "I'll have it ready for you when you come downstairs."

As he quickly retreated, Steve heard the bedroom door slam. Whistling to himself, he bounced merrily down the stairs.

An hour later, Cathy descended the staircase, looking poised and much calmer than when he had last seen her. The hot bath had soothed her temper.

Without realizing why, she had decided on an utterly feminine pale green silk dress with a subtle jacquard weave, the color accentuating the green flecks in her hazel eyes. Her hair was pulled back in its usual chignon. Small jade earrings were the only jewelry she wore.

Steve rose slowly from his chair. "My, my, what a good night's sleep will do for some people."

The look of approval on his face sent a pleasant feeling rushing through her, a feeling she accepted even while telling herself that his approval was of no importance to her.

"I do feel much better, thanks to your hospitality."

While bathing, Cathy had determined she would revert to her cool-lady image. No more yelling at him.

She took the coffee he offered her. No mug this time; the cup he handed her was delicate china.

"Thank you." Her voice was silky, calm.

Standing in front of her, he looked down, surveying every detail about her. She pretended not to notice.

"While you have your coffee, Cathy, I'll change. Then I'm going to take you to dinner. Food like you've never tasted in your life—you do like Italian, don't you?"

"Very much," she responded gracefully.

He was about to turn away, but then he stopped. "Cathy, one little thing."

"Yes?" She smiled politely.

"Why do you always wear your hair pulled back like that?"

She felt her poise slipping but, being in full control, she put her emotional brakes on. "Because I like it that way, Steve."

"Oh," he said dryly as he stooped over her. "Your hair smells wonderful."

Suspiciously, she retorted, "I just washed it."

"Well, I like it down much better."

Cathy felt the two small combs at the back of her head being pulled out and her hair falling in disarray around her shoulders.

"Damn you, Steve Bronsky! First you tell me where I'm going to sleep and now you want to tell me how to fix my hair!" She jumped up from the sofa, shoving him aside. "I'm getting out of here. Now."

"Please, Cathy. . .you can't just walk out on me," he pleaded.

"Watch me!"

She started toward the staircase but he grabbed her arm.

"Look, I'm sorry. I seem to have a knack for upsetting you. I apologize...really." There was no sign of forgiveness from her. "Cathy, would hitting me make you feel better?"

His hand still held tightly to her arm—very tightly. She turned quickly and was about to take him up on his suggestion, but in turning she came face-to-face with his pleading expression: those damnable brown eyes of his, those outrageously glowing pupils—and that mouth, so attractive with its sensual lips seemingly beckoning to her as they did before she had fallen asleep.

Steve must have seen something in Cathy's eyes as she looked at him. For a brief moment they were both silent. And then Cathy felt herself being pulled closer to him, closer to those eyes, to those lips. She felt his mouth touch hers, softly and tenderly, only a gentle brush at first; but in that brush, in the magical taste of his breath on hers, she felt an electric sensation surge across her skin, from her head to her toes, and as the current passed her heart, she felt it leap joyously.

With closed eyes she sensed some unknown force raise her arms and guide them around Steve's shoulders. His warmth caused excitement to flow wildly through her body as she stroked the back of his strong neck, as her fingers slid upward into his dark hair.

Still, his lips merely wandered slowly across hers as she felt his hands move to her back and begin a soothing movement, upward, downward; but then she felt his soft moan on her lips, felt his tongue slip past her lips, and then his mouth came down on hers, harder and harder as she arched her body against his solid, muscled form.

Just as a delightful dizziness threatened to overcome her, Steve pulled away, holding her at arm's length. She opened her eyes and found herself looking into his confused, blinking orbs.

"I'd better change." His voice was an apology.

Then he left her standing there in the middle of the living room, half-dazed, as he bounded up the stairs two at a time.

For a second she just stood there, wondering what had happened, wondering why he had stopped so suddenly, wondering why he had pushed her away. True, he had said she was no sex goddess, but why would he start something and break it off so suddenly?

She sat down on the sofa, trying to figure out if she should be angry or disappointed. The coffee was still warm, but it didn't help her decide. Seeing his cigarettes on the table, she lit one, took a puff, choked, and snuffed it out violently.

Steady, Catherine, she told herself, *you're leaving the main highway. Get yourself back on track. Remember, this is the man who never wanted you here in the first place. And now, what's he up to? It was a kiss—only a kiss—nothing more. He's a man and you're a woman. But it's never going to happen again.*

She raced up the stairway, but once in her bedroom, it never occurred to her to redo her hair in its usual chignon; instead, she brushed it until the flowing strands gained body and a silky gloss. Then, with a false sense of surety, she repacked her makeup case, knowing that she couldn't spend another night so close to Steve—not with the stirrings his kiss had awakened in her, deep, emotional stirrings that she had long ago forced from her consciousness.

When Steve came downstairs carrying his suit jacket, Cathy smiled as though nothing had happened between them. "Ready?" she asked blithely.

"Ready," he answered, a tautness still to be seen in the line of his jaw.

Standing in the foyer, he turned as he was about to open the front door. He looked at her, bewilderment—or was it hesitation?—in his eyes. "Cathy, I want to explain why—"

"Explain what?" she asked quietly. "We shared a kiss, a moment of intimacy...that's all. What's wrong with that? As long as no one gets hurt."

Steve leaned back against the wall, his eyes boring into hers, somewhat unsettled by her attitude of supposed indifference. "I don't want either one of us to get hurt. It won't happen again. I promise."

The sinking feeling deep in the pit of her stomach worsened. "I think that's wise, Steve. We do have a lot of work to do, don't we?"

"Yes, we do." His smile was forced but full of all the warmth that charmed her so. "And right now our job is to get some food into you." He opened the door; his arm swept out. "After you, Miss Arensen."

"Thank you, Mr. Bronsky," she mimicked, trying to match his smile.

Darkness had settled over the Village. The lampposts along the row of houses on St. Luke's Place gave the street a softness, an almost European charm. Steve took Cathy's arm as they crossed the street.

"Like to walk, Cathy? The restaurant's only a few blocks away."

"Love it. In California, instead of jogging, I try to walk a few miles every day."

"That's the only way to see Manhattan...on foot."

Sitting in the restaurant, Steve raised his wineglass. "Shall we try another 'Welcome to New York' and start all over again?"

This was all she needed, Cathy thought, a ruggedly handsome man toasting her with wine to the strains of soft, romantic music in the background. She lifted her glass and he touched his to hers.

"*Cin-cin*, Cathy. Welcome," he whispered.

She held her glass in midair, touching his, not being able to move her hand, nor did he move his. His eyes were searching hers and she felt powerless to look away.

"*Cin-cin*, Steve," she said quickly, and sipped the red wine.

As they progressed through dinner Steve turned the conversation to Cathy's past, listening intently as she spoke.

"After I finished high school in Wisconsin, I went to live with my aunt in Hollywood. I majored in journalism at UCLA."

"Why'd you leave Wisconsin? Seventeen is kind of young to go off on your own?" His question was innocent enough, and he was surprised to see Cathy's face darken.

"I wasn't on my own," she said a little curtly. "I stayed with my aunt." She paused a moment and then her voice softened. "I came from a very small town, Steve. Everybody knew everyone else's business. Small-town people can be cruel without meaning to be." Forcing a smile, she continued, "Anyway, I wanted to be a writer and my aunt was a writer...soap operas for radio, and then TV."

"Is that how you got started with 'Howardsville General'?"

In a roundabout way. My aunt Elizabeth would let me read the dialogue she'd written. She used me as a sounding board, and pretty soon I found myself getting caught up in the plots and in the characters' lives. She'd have sessions with other writers in her home and those people would argue about the story lines for their characters. This character would never do that, or that one's fan mail would crucify her if she had the abortion. They were like a group of gods deciding the fates of the people they wrote for. I was fascinated by the whole business of soaps, and my aunt soon had me doing dialogues part-time while I was still hammering away at journalism."

Steve twirled the wineglass between his fingers. "So, the bug bit you, too. I got into it for the money and soon found myself going through the same thing. Some people think soaps are totally unrealistic, but I know from personal experience that people do get into conflicts over their children, that marriage is difficult...losses are painful."

Cathy sensed that his sad tone came from the heart and not from some script about life. She tried to angle the conversation toward generalities. "And whether the detractors of soaps know it or not, it's the public that dictates the story lines. If the ratings drop—" She didn't finish. One look at Steve's face told her she had made her point. "Enough about business, Steve. Tomorrow's another day."

He tapped a cigarette and lit it, careful to blow the smoke to the side, away from her. "Going to move in with me, Cathy?"

She rested her elbows on the table, her chin barely touching her folded hands. Her every heartbeat wanted her to say *yes, yes, I will*, but her years of avoiding a true commitment to another human being answered for her.

"No, Steve...I'm not. I'm sure I can find something in Sunday's paper. I really don't need a big place. Just somewhere to—"

"Would you believe I'm starting to miss you already?" he interrupted. The sincerity in his voice was obvious, as was the look in his eyes. "Don't be misled, C.A. I'm rather particular about who I ask to live with me...even though I hate the loneliness of—" Silence, and then a quick puff.

Cathy wanted to tell him that she would miss being with him in his home; it was comfortable, physically and mentally, and even in the brief time she had been there, she actually felt she belonged there with him; but the intimate proximity signaled danger to her, so she said nothing.

After dinner they walked awhile. The narrow streets of the Village were fairly crowded; and as they walked she examined the small old red-brick houses with their fine ironwork on the railings and fences, deciding that the basement restaurants gave the section a nineteenth-century charm.

As they approached Washington Square, the lights form the white balls high atop the lampposts surrounding the square gave off an eerie glow that made the Washington Arch look like an old Roman edifice. The square was crowded with people of all types, some shirtless, some in cocktail outfits. A small ensemble was playing baroque music; the flutist, a young woman, executed her runs and trills with clean precision.

Steve stopped before they hit the main crowd. Cathy felt his hand slide up her arm, his fingers press into her bare skin. She wanted to tell him to stop, but she didn't want him to realize his touch bothered her so.

The night air was warm, and Cathy realized she was perspiring when she ran her fingers across her forehead. Then a warm breeze brushed across her face. Looking up at the starless night, she saw a mass of low-lying clouds rushing across the skyscrapers of Manhattan.

"Looks like rain, Steve. Think we should start back?" she asked, wanting to retreat to the privacy of her bedroom.

"I think you're right." He glanced upward at the clouds and then over at her. "Do you like rain?"

"Only if I'm inside where it's dry," she told him, wondering why he was smiling.

"I like rain. It cleans the air and cools things off."

Suddenly the wind strengthened and Cathy could hear the leaves rustling in the trees overhead.

"Steve, the leaves are trying to tell us something. I'm sure it's going to rain."

"Right. C'mon, let's head home."

"Are we going to walk back?" she asked, smelling the rain in the air.

"Do you have any idea what it's like trying to get a cab in New York when it's raining? Besides, we're not that far away."

He took her hand and started walking southwest with long strides, forcing Cathy to walk faster than she did when she took her daily walks in California.

They were just crossing Bleecker Street when the rain came, pelting them with huge drops. In moments, Cathy's hair was falling in wet strands over her forehead, her green silk dress clinging to her body. At Seventh Avenue, Steve removed his jacket and placed it around her shoulders.

"That better?" His smile made him look like a pleased little boy.

"Oh, wonderful, just wonderful," she tossed back at him, annoyed that he looked like he was enjoying the deluge. "Are we almost there?"

"Just around the corner." He pulled back on her hand as she started to trot off in the direction she thought his house was located. "What's the rush? We're already soaked," he told her, laughing at the upset he saw in her eyes, and then, guiding her in the opposite direction, "No. . .this way. C'mon."

He took her hand again and began a slow gait around the corner, tilting his head upward to catch the rain.

Cathy glanced over at him, not believing what she saw. He was actually enjoying being rained on. His dark wavy hair lay soaked against his forehead, but it didn't seem to faze him; he was smiling with closed eyes, dragging her along next to him as though it were a clear, sunlit spring day.

She felt clumsy and awkward trying to keep his wet jacket on her shoulders as the rain and her long straight strands of soaked hair all but obliterated her view. And then she started to slip on the wet pavement, the heels of her shoes being higher than the ones she usually wore.

"Take them off," he suggested.

"And walk barefoot? Are you crazy?" she sputtered, the rain dripping from her nose onto her lips as she spoke.

"The sidewalks are washed now. What's the problem?" Another slip, but his firm hold on her kept her from falling. "Give 'em to me. I'll carry them."

They stopped and Cathy balanced herself by holding on to his shoulder, feeling his solid body and his warm skin through his wet dress shirt.

"This is definitely not my idea of fun, Steve. I thought you said we were almost there."

"Just around the corner and we will be."

He took her shoes. She just stood there, the rain pelting the two of them.

"Around the corner?"

"That's right."

"We'll be right back where we started. Why didn't we go around the other way? Wouldn't it have been shorter?"

"Yes, but you would have missed all this. Haven't you ever walked in the rain before?"

She felt her blood begin to boil. "Steve, I think your brain's gone bye-bye!"

As she was about to add further insult she saw the corners of his eyes narrow and his mouth try to suppress a smile that made her melt inside. The rain dribbled over his long lashes onto his cheekbones and down onto his chin as he angled his head to give her an intimate look. The rain had plastered his shirt against his skin, too clearly defining the finely sculptured physique that had already received too much of her attention.

Then Cathy felt her own facial muscles relax and heard herself join the low chuckle he tried unsuccessfully to control. His mirth grew between staccato breaths, and as his lips spread, exposing his beautiful white teeth, her own laughter matched his until they were both shaking with raucous howls, oblivious to the rain that continued to drench them.

As Steve calmed down, Cathy saw that he was eyeing her silk dress. She knew it was clinging to her as his shirt was to him. Her own laughter stopped when she saw the serious glimmer in his eyes, saw his lashes blink away the rain.

"Cathy, I—" He stopped in mid-sentence as his hands reached for her.

Closing his jacket around her, she took a step backward, only to find herself up against a wrought-iron fence. The pounding of her heart mixed with a distant clap of thunder as he moved closer.

Looking up into the rain-washed face closing in on her, she again felt the repressed desires surge through her body. Even in the rain, she caught a whiff of that pleasant lime odor she had first come across when her head had lain on his pillow; even in the rain the glow of his skin and eyes made her want to touch his cheek. His face was so close now.

"Steve—"

His lips muffled her next word and his arms pressed her to him with such force that she thought all her breath had left her. As his jacket slipped from her shoulders and fell to the pavement, she felt the rain running down her back, under the low, rounded collar of her dress.

Through the sopped material of their clothes, she could feel her breasts rubbing against his solid chest as his hands moved down her back, lower and lower, pressing her tightly against his muscled thighs.

Again, the sound of thunder. Cathy pulled her mouth from his, and as her head tilted backward, the rain cascaded down her face. His warm mouth was at her neck; she arched her head sideways, feeling his hot breath as he trailed kisses down her throat toward her breasts.

The weight of him against her forced her backward to the iron fence behind her. She felt a sharp pain from the hard metal and uttered a low moan. He stopped and pulled her away from the fence.

"Are you hurt?" His voice was all concern, as were his eyes.

"No," she murmured, suddenly feeling very silly standing in the rain. Looking at Steve, she wasn't sure if she was going to laugh or cry; she wanted to do both. Instead, she moved slowly away, barefoot, running her fingers along the wrought iron. Turning, she saw that he was just standing there in the rain, watching her. "But, you know what, Steve?"

"What?" he asked, staring at her with inquisitive eyes.

Cathy looked skyward, the rain still falling on her face. "Behind those clouds up there, I bet there's a full moon tonight."

"That's bringing out the wolf in me, you mean?"

"In both of us, perhaps."

Carefully, Steve bent down and picked up the jacket that had fallen from her shoulders. He offered it to her, but Cathy shook her head in refusal. After picking up the shoes he had dropped, he extended his wet hand and waited for her to walk back to him, which she did, placing her hand in his.

Without speaking, they walked down the street in the rain, turned the corner, and were home.

Chapter Four

Steve unlocked the door and Cathy hurried inside. In moments, a puddle formed around her bare feet on the black-and-white linoleum floor.

"Now what?" she asked as he closed the door behind him and slipped the dead bolt shut.

"Now we get out of these wet clothes, that's what."

"Steve, we'll ruin the carpets."

"Not to worry...polyester, Scotch Guard...the whole bit."

The antique wall clock hanging over the marble-topped credenza in the foyer struck ten as he took her hand and led her up the carpeted stairs.

After a quick shower, she towel-dried her hair and made a turban for it with a smaller white one. She was tempted to put on her very feminine blue robe, but second thoughts dictated her loose-fitting white terry cloth.

As Cathy started down the stairs, she heard soft piano music coming from the stereo—Chopin Preludes. Steve was standing barefoot by the wall unit, his back to her, wearing a short brown velour robe. It was impossible for her not to notice his long, muscular legs, legs which she assumed had run many a mile across a football field. She forced her eyes to look away just as he turned around.

In one long gaze, he studied the robe, the turbaned head. ''You look good in white. . .make a fabulous bride.''

Cathy hesitated a moment, then smiled. ''Is that a proposal, Bronsky?'' Quickly followed by, ''Forget I said that.''

''Sit,'' he ordered, handing her a small liqueur glass.

''What am I drinking?'' she asked cautiously.

''Calvados. I don't want my supervising producer off nursing a cold.''

Cathy sniffed its fragrance. ''Apple?''

''Apple brandy.'' Holding up his glass, he toasted, ''Cheers.''

''Whew!'' followed her first sip. ''That'll clear your sinuses.''

''Also cures dropsy and elephantiasis. . .if you drink enough of it.''

Cathy smiled and shook her head. ''You're crazy, you know that, don't you?''

''The whole world's going crazy. Why should I be different?''

''The whole world, Steve?''

Sitting down across from her, he saw her face freeze, and then quickly he pushed the ends of his robe down between his thighs. "Sorry about that"—his face showed his embarrassment—"but I guess I'm not used to a female roommate."

Nervously, she sipped on her Calvados. "It's not that I'm a prude, Steve, but I've never roomed with a man before."

He leaned forward. "Never?"

She wasn't certain just what he was asking. "I said I never roomed with a man, Steve. *Roomed.*"

He gave a low laugh and leaned back in his chair.

"What's so funny about that, may I ask?"

"Funny? Nothing. Remember, I'm crazy. You said so yourself."

"Well, sometimes you certainly act like you're not playing with a full deck."

Again he started to chuckle. Cathy saw him trying to control himself, but the more she watched in disbelief, the redder his face became until he finally burst out in healthy laughter.

"What is the matter with you, Steve? Are you hearing voices or something?"

The more he laughed, the more annoyed she became.

"No...no," he tried to answer, almost strangling on his words.

"Well, what the hell are you laughing about?"

Complete seriousness dominated his features. "For a minute there, I thought I was stuck with a middle-aged prude." And then he started again, forced to hold his sides for the pain he was going through as his laughter vibrated throughout the room.

Cathy slammed her glass on the table next to her and jumped up. "You...you...oh! I am *not* middle-aged, I am *not* a prude, and you are damn well not *stuck* with me!'' She stormed from the room and started up the stairs.

He called up after her, ''Hey, where are you going?''

Midway up she stopped, placed her slender fingers on the railing, and glared at him. ''To dry my hair,'' she said calmly.

Alone, Steve went to the portable bar cart and poured himself another Calvados. ''Steve boy. . .you've got to straighten up.'' His self-criticism was quickly followed by several deep chuckles.

In the bathroom, Cathy put the blower on high and waved it furiously over her hair. ''Stuck with me, huh!. . .oh, that—'' Feeling her head heat up, she switched the blower to cool and slowed her hand motions.

When her hair was dry she began to brush it. Her face was still flushed from his remark. ''Middle-aged prude!'' She slammed her brush down. ''The nerve of that—''

If someone had asked her why she reached for her perfume and dabbed it behind her ears, she would have denied doing so, but she did do it.

''I'll show him I'm not flustered that easily,'' she said as she made her way back to the living room.

Halfway down the stairs she forced a pleasant smile; she all but floated down the remaining steps, just the way she remembered seeing Katharine Hepburn do in an old move on TV. She was determined to be sophisticated, ladylike, and worldly—just like Miss Hepburn.

Steve raised both palms up toward Cathy. ''Truce. . .okay?''

''Whatever do you mean, Steve?'' She even sounded like Hepburn.

"Well, I do have a slight problem with my sense of humor. I've been told that by others, believe it or not."

Cathy reached for her liqueur glass and glanced at him *à la* Hepburn. "Oh, I believe it, Steve, but that's your problem, isn't it?"

Cocking his head, he looked at her strangely, seeing and hearing something different about her. "What's wrong with your voice?"

"Why, nothing...nothing at all. What makes you ask?" she inquired, nervously swinging her crossed foot under the long terry-cloth robe.

"Oh, nothing. I guess I'm imagining things again."

"You're quite good at that, aren't you, Steve?"

He carried his glass to the stereo and turned the cassette over. When he returned he started to sit down next to her on the sofa.

"Over there," she ordered in her Cathy Arensen voice, her finger indicating the easy chair across from her.

He smiled knowingly and nodded his head. "Now that we're all calm and being very adult," he began, the epitome of the mature male, "we should discuss the ground rules while you're living here."

Miss Hepburn replied, "I haven't said I was going to live here, Steve. You've got to learn to listen when people talk to you."

"But you *do* see that it makes a lot of sense, don't you?" Now he sounded as though he were talking to a child.

"A lot of sense to whom, Steve?"

"To whom?" he repeated, wondering who wasn't listening now. "To both of us." He smiled apologetically. "Dopey me, I thought I had made that clear. I mean about all the work we have to do...together...the after-hours work. . .together. All the cab rides we could avoid. Remember, Cathy, New York is not a safe place for a young, attractive girl like you to be roaming around in all by herself.''

''I can take care of myself, Steve.''

''Oh, I'm sure you can, but I feel kind of responsible for you.''

''You are *not* responsible for me, Steve.'' She almost shouted across at him.

''You're right. . .definitely right. I just meant that since you'll be working for me—''

''Reread my contract, Steve. We are working *together*. I wouldn't have touched this job if I hadn't been given certain powers to do my work as I see it.'' Now she had him in a corner and she was going to nail him. ''You've been a paragon in this business, Steve, but for the last year you've been screwing up, and it's my job to find out what's wrong and get you back on course.''

If Cathy had slapped him in the face, she could have understood the look on the man across from her. The usually shiny eyes dulled before her; the mouth, usually angled in a smile, sagged. The quiet in the room seemed interminable. When Steve did speak, his voice was low, with no trace of humor.

''Cathy. . .when you work with the cast and writers, you might want to try putting a velvet glove on that iron fist of yours.''

She bit her lip and then ran her hand along the side of her neck. ''I'm sorry. There were other ways I could have said what I just did.''

He finished his drink in one swallow and then leaned forward, resting his arms on his knees. "Whoever said that the truth hurts knew what he was talking about."

She leaned against the sofa and propped one elbow on the back of it, resting her head against her curved hand. "And it is the truth, Steve. The ratings are causing your sponsors to run, not walk, to other soaps. A lot of people are going to be on the unemployment line if we don't find out what went wrong this year."

"Don't you think you've got a better chance of finding out if you're with me day and night?"

Now Cathy leaned forward, seriousness and sincerity punctuating her every word. "Steve, if I were to live here with you there'd be a better chance of a lot of things happening."

"Such as?"

Should she tell him? she wondered; should she let him know how attracted she was to him? Already there were two episodes behind them, two intimate encounters, and those in only twenty-four hours. Already she was frightened by the normal desires he had awakened in her, desires she had pounded down into her unconscious for a very good reason, she thought. Reality—she must now think reality, she told herself.

"Steve, in case you hadn't noticed, I'm a woman and you're a man. Although I'm not a sex goddess, as you were quick to point out, if I were to live here, it would be very convenient for you to—"

"To what, Cathy? To make love to you? If that's what's worrying you, you can forget it. I've no interest in love. Not anymore. And," he added firmly, "I'm very capable of controlling myself."

"I wish I could say the same." There, it was out and she was glad of it.

The tautness that had gripped Steve's face for the past few minutes was suddenly lifted by the light that glowed in his eyes, a light that spread across his cheeks and raised the corners of his mouth. "Cathy, I've got years on you." He laughed quietly. "In fact, tomorrow is the big four-oh."

"Your birthday?"

"Yes, you know…thirty-nine, forty."

"Steve, you're a handsome man. Time has only fine-tuned your attractiveness." She believed every word she uttered. "And I'll be thirty-two on my next birthday." *What am I saying?* she asked herself. *It's going to sound to him like I'm selling myself…like I want an involvement.* "What I mean is, the proximity of two healthy, uncommitted adults living together is asking for trouble."

"Remember 'Three's Company,'" he suggested.

"I'm talking real life, not a TV program."

Getting up, he moved directly in front of her, looking down at her with eyes once again shining brightly. "Cathy, give it a chance—a month, a week—that's all I'm asking. If it doesn't work out we say so, and I swear to God, I'll even help you find a place…help you move out."

He leaned closer to her, resting one hand on the arm of the sofa. Cathy's eyes blinked nervously. His chest was directly in her line of vision; her eyes couldn't help but scan the firm, tanned flesh splashed with fine, wavy brown hair. And again, that lime fragrance.

It seemed to her that he was moving closer and closer. Her hand went up and pressed against his chest to move him away. "Steve, I need some breathing space…please."

He didn't move. "You can have breathing space or anything else you want."

Her palm remained on his chest and it burned with the feel of him. "Right now I want you to back off...back away so I can think clearly," she said firmly.

Steve swung his body down next to her on the sofa. He sat close, letting his bare knee lean against her robed one. "Yes, it's important we both think clearly. After all, living together is making a kind of commitment, isn't it?" He searched her face for some clue to her feelings at the moment. "And we have decided we're both attracted to each other, haven't we?"

Her eyes angled a quick look at him. "Are you saying you're attracted to me?"

"You don't think I go around indiscriminately kissing girls in the rain, do you?"

"I wouldn't put it past you, but that's exactly what I'm driving at. I just happened to be there when you felt like kissing someone."

"And you're afraid to be near if I should suddenly be overwhelmed by more basic urges. Is that it?"

Her hands crossed and she hugged her arms. "Something like that," she murmured.

"Cathy," he started slowly, "I said I could control myself, but you seem to have some reservations about doing the same. Maybe it's *your* being overwhelmed by *your* basic urges that's worrying you."

With that she jumped up and began pacing. "I am not about to discuss my basic urges with you, Steve. In fact, I hate this entire conversation we're having."

"Okay, okay. Back to ground rules. No smoking in bed."

"I don't smoke at all."

"No bringing friends home for dinner without prior warning."

"I'm not ill-mannered, Steve."

"No going to bed without kissing the other good night."

"Without saying good night," she corrected him.

"Well," he said happily, "that settles that. You're staying."

The single clap of his hands was followed by an icy stare from Cathy. "On one condition," she said quickly.

He stood up. "Name it."

She looked him square in the eye. "From now on you promise to wear shorts under that robe of yours."

"Party pooper," he said, his eyes never leaving hers.

"I'm not here for a party, Steve. We've got an uphill road ahead. Both of our careers are on the line, and it's not going to be a party for either one of us."

"The voice of reason speaks...and wisely." He reached for her glass and held it up.

"No, Steve. I'm going to call it a day. I want to get an early start tomorrow."

"We're going to work on my birthday?" he asked sullenly.

She had already started toward the stairs; she stopped, turned. "Might be good for you. Help you get by the big four-oh."

Their mutual smiles said more than was needed. As Cathy started up to her bedroom, Steve moved to the bottom of the staircase. Looking up at her with light in his eyes, he called, "Cathy." And then he said quietly, "Sleep well."

She looked down at him over her shoulder, letting a sigh slip through her lips. "Good night."

Her bedroom door seemed far away, but she directed her steps straight for it, and only inside the privacy of her room did she finally relax.

After switching off the lamp on her night table, she sank back into the pillow, thinking momentarily just how familiar the room had become to her: the yellow brocade draperies, the set of Utrillo lithographs over the headboard. She felt comfortable and safe here with Steve just down the hall. Or was she safe? Did she really want to be safe?

Almost angry with herself for having such thoughts, she turned over on her stomach and punched her pillow as though to punish it. After all, she told herself, she was not an unthinking adolescent. She had always managed to control her emotions—well, almost always, except for that one time, and she had paid dearly for that one indiscretion. Since that time she had set her life on a course without serious entanglements, given her strengths to her career, and nothing and no one was going to alter that.

Still reassuring herself, Cathy slowly drifted off to sleep with fractured visions of Steve's laughter and his strange sadness. Her sleep was deep, so deep that she never heard the door to her bedroom being opened, nor did she feel the soft kiss that touched her hair.

At six-thirty Sunday morning, Cathy's clock radio let loose with the brassy sound of one of the big bands of the forties. Her hand shot out and slapped the snooze button on top. "I'm going to have to adjust that," she mumbled.

Languidly she worked her way up to a sitting position, stretched, and fluffed her hair. Then, seeing her door open, she began to rethink her movements of the night before. She was certain she had closed it. "Circulation," she said out loud. "God forbid I shouldn't have good air circulation."

Following her usual morning ritual, Cathy debated on which robe to wear. She decided on the ultrafeminine blue silk. Just as she started to leave the room, she heard music and went back to shut off her clock radio, which she thought she had already done. She had. Then she realized the music was coming from downstairs.

Halfway down, she stopped. Something was odd about the music she heard. A trained soprano voice was singing a supersaccharine waltz. She knew Steve was into classical music, but what pelted her ears was ridiculous.

"Well, good afternoon, slugabed," he welcomed her, handing her a large glass of what looked like tomato juice.

"Slugabed? It's not even seven yet." She took the glass.

"I thought you said you wanted to get an *early* start."

"I hadn't planned on beating the sun up." One sip of her tomato juice and her nose wrinkled. "I think this juice is over the hill, Steve. It's got a strange taste."

"Beer."

"Beer?"

"Just a little beer mixed with the tomato juice."

"At seven in the morning?"

"Why not? Besides, it's a ritual with me...every Sunday morning. Beer and tomato juice while I listen to *Little Mary Sunshine*. You know, the famous Broadway musical that catapulted Eileen Brennan to fame and made her a household word."

"*Little Mary Sunshine*?" she repeated dubiously, sitting as far away from the stereo as possible, trying to drink her tomato juice.

Steve turned the volume down. "Oh come on...it's got one of the greatest plots ever conceived."

"Which is?"

"Mary makes her living selling her cookies to the Forest Rangers."

The messy spurt of beer and tomato juice spotted the carefully chosen blue robe in a matter of seconds. "Damn!" she blurted out, jumping up and rushing toward the stairs, still holding her half-full glass. "I've got to rinse this"—she thrust the glass at him—"this...here, you finish it!"

Steve watched her race up the stairs, shaking his head sideways. Luckily, she was out of earshot when he said, "You're a strange one, Cathy Arensen."

When Cathy returned wearing her white terry cloth, she warned him. "One word about looking like a bride and you'll never drink tomato juice again."

His hands went up in an acquiescent gesture. Then, he said, "C'mon. I need your help."

She followed him into the kitchen—not a large space, but ultramodern and roomy enough. Either he was very neat or he didn't use it very often, she guessed. One look toward the stove, though, and she decided he knew what he was doing. There was a fluffy omelet folded over with red sauce oozing out, and there was a definite smell of sausage.

"There." He pointed to a carafe of hot coffee. "Take that into the dining room and light the candle under the stand. Matches are on the table. Be right there."

"Yes sir," she said crisply, obediently taking the hot coffee.

Another first view—the dining room. The door had been closed until this morning; Cathy hadn't been sure what was on the other side. It paralleled the living room and also opened out onto the back garden, which she could see through closed French doors.

The room was charming. Under a curved brass-and-wood chandelier was a highly polished oval cherrywood table that could comfortably seat six. Only two of the antique chairs were placed at the table, which Steve had set with great care. A large tapestry depicting two lovers resting under the shade of a willow tree hung over a long side buffet.

Cathy lit the candle and placed the carafe on its stand, as instructed, just as Steve came in carrying two plates.

"Sit, sit!" he commanded, putting a plate before her and then pouring her coffee.

"I'm impressed," she said sincerely. "You're too good a find to be running around loose, Steve."

A strange smile set on his lips, but quickly disappeared. "I'll buy that. Now, eat before it gets cold." He started to sit down, but then remembered. "The toast! Be right back." He was off again, but in seconds he was back with a plate of hot toast.

Breakfast conversation was general, about California, about New York, and it was not until Cathy asked if he had supervised the decorating of his home that his eyes lost some of their sparkle.

"No, I can't take credit for that. I had a lot of help." He placed his napkin down, seeing that she, too, had finished. "Take your coffee inside and I'll get this straightened up."

"Oh, no you don't. We're in this thing together, and I'll do my share of the work around here." She took the plate he had already picked up.

"What do you think this is, lady. . .my birthday or something?"

And then it dawned on her—it *was* his birthday.

"Oh, Steve, I'm sorry. I did forget. Happy birthday."

"It's gonna cost you." He leaned his cheek toward her and smiled after she kissed him. "Now, that makes having a birthday worthwhile."

Cathy whizzed through the dishes, examining the cupboards to see what went where. Then, feeling a little odd about doing so, she looked in the refrigerator and freezer to see what kind of supplies were on hand. A trip to the store was a must, she decided.

Leaving the kitchen, Cathy found that Steve wasn't in the living room. A glance toward the study told her the light was on in there.

"Steve."

"In here."

Cathy stopped at the door to the study, watching Steve setting up an easel on the far side of the room. She looked at the desk, previously piled high with stacks of papers and files. But now everything was order personified. The scripts were piled in neat stacks on the long side table and the budget material was now in marked manila folders on the desk.

"Didn't you go to bed at all last night, Steve?"

"Don't I look rested?"

"You look hyperactive."

"You *said* you liked order." Pointing to the desk, "*Voilà*."

He reached behind the easel for a large poster board and set it up for her inspection. It was covered with eight-by-ten photos.

"The cast of 'Search for Love,'" she exclaimed.

"Only those who have story lines. It helps me when I check what the writers are planning to do with these people."

Cathy ran a finger across her chin. "We've got to get one of Devlin up there."

"You're really sold on him, aren't you?"

"When you find someone like Devlin, you use him."

Steve started to say something, but decided against it. Instead, he went to the desk. "The master sheets, showing which actor is scheduled to be in the studio on which day, are here." He indicated one of the folders. "The schedules for the line rehearsals, the blockings, and the run-throughs on sets are in here. I keep the long-term story projections in this looseleaf. They've been changing a lot recently."

"You have been busy," she praised.

"The technicians' schedule is in here. You already know we shoot in two shifts. Call for the morning shift is seven, afternoon is two. We try like hell to see that actors don't have to work both shifts, but sometimes—"

"Tell me about it." She chuckled. "They're either thrilled with the exposure or they hate your guts for interfering with their private lives."

Steve sat in his desk chair and leaned back. Cathy made herself comfortable, sitting on the edge of the large desk, crossing her legs, which Steve's eyes didn't fail to notice.

"That Vanessa, though," he said, "what a dream. She'd be there till midnight if you needed her."

Cathy leaned toward him. "Steve, I wanted to talk to you about Vanessa. She's played a witch so long—"

"And successfully, don't forget that."

"I know, but from the tapes I've seen, I think she's got a lot more to her than that one-dimensional characterization."

"Try to change that and she'll fight you all the way, Cathy."

"I expect that, but once she realizes that her character could be made a little more complicated, more—" Her hand went up in exasperation. "Steve, the audience wants to know why villains are the way they are. They want to understand, and I think Vanessa's fans would enjoy seeing what makes her tick, more than just watching her tick away…and to show them, we've got to develop other parts of her personality."

"I agree with you, but I know Vanessa."

Cathy cupped her knee with her braided fingers. "Steve, I'm not comfortable wearing velvet gloves, as you suggested, and I'm not here to win a personality award. You know as well as I do that young people now make up more than half of the soap opera audience. Look at the other soaps. Who are the new vixens? They're young girls."

She walked to the easel and pointed out two girls in their late teens. "Look at the Rubin sisters, Dianne and Lilly. Lilly came on board as a sweet young thing, but it's Dianne, who's been cast as a real bitch, that's going to get the attention of the audience…and Vanessa is going to have cardiac arrest once she realizes the competition Dianne is going to give her if Vanessa sees herself as only a vixen."

Steve leaned his elbow on the desk and nestled his chin in his hand. An understanding lit up his eyes. "You're really concerned about her, aren't you? That's why you want to give her a broader characterization."

"She's paid her dues, Steve. She deserves a little guidance *and* protection from us. . .and it'll be good for the show. I'm not talking about working toward sainthood for her, but just to tell the writers we want the audience to know she's a woman who's had things happen to her emotions that make her do the wrong things. Sure she hurts other people. . .but let's let the viewer know she herself hurts as well."

"Sounds good to me, Cathy. We'll give it a try. Talk to Dorothy in the morning."

Walking around to the front of the desk, Cathy leaned her hands on its edge. "Steve, I want to bring in a new head writer—Holly Lange. I've already talked to her about it, but told her I needed to check it out with you."

"And what do we do with Dorothy? Put her in a canoe, set it on fire, and push it out toward the sunset?"

Cathy winced at his insinuation that she was cold-hearted. She had spent her days in California meeting men in the industry head-on, and it hadn't fazed her, but with Steve it was different. She already knew he could hurt her with just a look. She reached for the pile of folders and flipped through them, took one, opened it, and threw it down in front of him.

"The latest Nielsen figures. Read and weep, Steve." She hurriedly looked through the other marked folders and pulled the recent budget figures out. Tossing that in front of him also, she continued, "Costs per week to produce 'SFL' are going right through the roof." The look on his face didn't make it any easier for her, but she wasn't going to stop now. "Everyone, Steve—*everyone*—has to pull his own weight around here, and Dorothy isn't doing that. 'SFL' has a snail's pace of storytelling. It's ho-hum time on paper. The actors can do just so much! She's been filling the tube with outmoded old soap images of men and women, not today's people.''

"Cathy, Dorothy is—''

"I've talked to the other writers, Steve. They've all come down with turmoil-at-the-typewriter. You and I can't be everywhere, do everything. We need a competent head writer to help us with the load we're carrying.''

He closed the folders and tossed them aside. "And you think Holly Lange can do it.''

Softening her tone, she said, "I know she can do it. I've worked with her often enough, in many situations, to see the ability she has to translate ideas and concepts onto the printed page, and she's got a knack for getting loyalty from her scritpers, for holding on to them. And Dorothy? Steve, her writers have changed so frequently in recent months that your cast aren't sure what kind of characters they're supposed to be playing. Their characterizations change with each new writer. You've had characters scripted to take a short trip, and then they're never heard from again. True, that happens on all soaps, but not with the frequency it has on 'SFL.' ''

Cathy watched as Steve tugged at his earlobe.

"One of these days, Steve, you're going to pull that ear right off your head.''

He stopped tugging. "You know, Cathy, the trouble with 'SFL' is not all Dorothy's fault. As the saying goes''—he thumped the top of his desk—"the buck stops here.''

"I know that," she said quietly, "but apparently Dorothy needs a strong overseer.''

"Which she hasn't had lately,'' he added.

Cathy crossed her arms. "I have a feeling that when 'SFL' was high in the charts, you were doing a lot of what Dorothy should have been doing. Oh," she moaned, "I'm not out to get Dorothy. I just honestly believe Holly would do a better job."

Steve looked up at Cathy, and for a moment he thought he saw the well-tailored lady with horn-rimmed glasses, her hair held back severely from her face. "They said you were sharp, C.A., and tough." His tone didn't tell her whether it was a compliment or a caustic remark. Then, he added, "Your contract gives you the right to change staff. Thanks for talking it over with me first."

"Steve, my contract only—"

"And what about me? Should I stay?" He wasn't being humorous.

"Steve, you've *been* 'SFL' for the past seven years. You're the one who made it climb toward the stars, and you kept it there even with murderous competition. It's just been this past year that something's gone sour, that things have gotten shaky."

"Then you're not going to fire me?" Now he was joking, knowing her powers didn't go that far.

Cathy walked around to his side of the desk, put her hands on his shoulders, and kissed his forehead. "On your birthday?"

"Birthday!" he gasped. "Oh, that reminds me." He got up quickly. "I've got some shopping to do if we're going to have a party tonight."

"Don't you want me to go with you?"

"Really, Miss Arensen. I *can* tell the difference between canned Spam and canned dog food. You just sit down there and pour through those story projections. Start earning your money. Whose birthday is this, anyway?''

"It's yours, Mr. Bronsky, and you're forty, forty, *forty*.''

He stopped at the doorway. "Thanks, I needed that.'' Then he left Cathy to begin sifting through the mounds of proposed plot ideas and scripts for the coming months.

Hours passed, during which she waded through a hodgepodge of happenings: kidnappings, alcoholism, spies, business mergers, jealousies, murders, miraculous returns of people thought dead, amnesia, divorces, illegitimate births, and even a proposed visitation by an alien being, a hunk who couldn't adjust to wearing clothes on earth, a proposal Steve had sensibly vetoed in red.

"Where?" Cathy moaned out load. "Where is the romance, the love that makes dealing with all this stuff bearable?" She took a swallow of the soda she had gotten from the refrigerator. "Holly, do we ever need you!"

After making copious notes to take with her to the meeting she had with the writers Monday morning, Cathy began pages of additional notes that she would use at her meetings with the directors, costume designers, the makeup artists and hair stylists, the music composers, the cast, and the woman who represented Broadcast Standards and Practices.

So much for Monday's schedule, she thought, as she heard the clock in the foyer chime three times. She took her empty drink can to the kitchen and disposed of it and then returned to the study to gather the notes she had made. Leaving Steve's desk as neat as she had found it that morning, Cathy took her notes to her bedroom and placed them in her attaché case.

On her way downstairs she had to pass Steve's room. She stopped for a moment outside his opened door and then peeked inside. His room was larger than hers and had the biggest bed she had ever seen, although she assumed all king-size beds were the same size. His just looked bigger to her.

The decor suited him, she thought, brown, tan, and gold, more masculine than her room. At first she just poked her head inside the doorframe, but then she eased herself inside the room, taking in the two large chests and the bureau, all the epitome of neatness. She ran her fingers down the slats of one of the wall-to-wall louvered closet doors, almost imagining him opening and closing them. As she passed his bureau, she picked up his brush knowing that he had probably touched it that morning.

Then, feeling very much like an intruder, she glanced inside his bathroom. Spotless. "God, he's neat," she said to herself. And there on the side of the vanity she saw his bottle of after-shave. She reached for it and, unscrewing the top, she inhaled deeply.

"Anyone home?" came his voice from downstairs.

Cathy almost dropped the bottle as she hurriedly screwed the top on and dashed for the hallway, poising herself at the top of the stairs.

"I was beginning to think you had started your birthday celebration without me," she said casually, knowing that *she* could still smell the aroma of lime in her nostrils, but praying that he wouldn't.

"Not a chance. Here, take these into the kitchen. I've still got some packages in the cab outside."

She took two packed grocery bags from him and he left again. In the kitchen she decided to wait for him to put things away. It was his kitchen and he knew where he wanted things to go.

When Steve returned, he was carrying a large white box with a bakery name on it and another large box wrapped in birthday paper and fitted with a large brown bow.

"Your birthday present to me," he informed her, putting the wrapped package on a table in the living room. "And this"—he showed her the bakery box—"I'll put in the dining room so you can light the candles later and surprise me." He stopped at the dining room door. "You do know the words to 'Happy Birthday,' don't you?"

Her smile came easily. "Yes, I know the words." But inside she felt a little sad that he had had to arrange his own birthday celebration, and she wondered if she were not there, would he have celebrated it at all?

Steve came back to the living room and let his body fall onto the sofa. "Well, I think that's everything. Did you find yourself something for lunch?"

"Found a soda and a tin of sardines in tomato sauce. I wasn't sure if you were ever coming back."

"Put any beer in the tomato sauce?"

"Yuck! I bet you pour beer over ice cream."

A look of wonderment formed on his face. "You know, you may have just hit on a new gourmet delight." He kicked off his loafers. "Why is it that at thirty-nine I felt twenty, and at forty I feel sixty?"

Cathy arched her elbow and pretended to play an imaginary violin. "Are you looking for sympathy?"

"No. I was hoping you'd offer to get me a beer."

"Right away, boss. Have you had lunch?" she asked on her way to the kitchen.

"Nope. I'm saving my appetite for the delicious dinner I'm going to fix."

He heard the pop-top snap on the beer and then saw her head appear in the doorway. "What's with you, Bronsky? Afraid to eat *my* cooking?" Before he could answer, she asked, "Want a glass?"

"Can's fine."

She held out the beer for him to take. "Do you trust me to put the groceries away, Steve?"

"Well, you certainly don't think I'm going to do *everything* around here, do you?"

With hands on her hips, she was about to spout off.

"Uh-uh." He cocked his head. "It's my birthday."

"Something tells me I'm going to be glad to see this day go by," she admitted, retreating to the kitchen.

Steve placed a cassette in the stereo, soothing background music, and then lay down on the sofa, his beer on the floor within easy reach. When Cathy did return, she took her soda and curled up in the easy chair across from him.

"Steve, what do you think about putting Ted in a coma for a while?"

"Cathy, I'm not *that* mad at the guy."

"Oh, be serious. He's really causing problems on the set."

"Write in a car accident?"

"Why not?"

Steve looked over at her. Sitting in the big chair, she seemed so petite, so sweet, but she made decisions like a driven Valkyrie. "So we lose Mr. Beefcake," he said slowly. "Let me guess the rest of it. Where would we ever get another hunk to parade around in Jockey shorts?" He sat upright. "Do you think you could *possibly* talk Devlin into undressing for the camera?"

Cathy watched his performance with interest. "What's wrong with the idea?" she asked dryly. "We get rid of a pain, temporarily, and we give the female audience someone to drool over."

"But can the guy act?"

"Who cares! No. . .I don't mean that. What I mean is. . .well, take that line Ted spit out in ten seconds. Devlin took it and with sensitive pauses and creating his own actions, that ten seconds ran to almost a minute and a half. That's time, Steve, and money. . .and time well spent, I might add. Did you get the look on Vanessa's face when he finished with her. And she's no ingénue."

"Of course those violet-blue eyes have nothing to do with your having discovered a new star," he added sarcastically.

"They have everything to do with it. Steve, I'm a woman and our audience is made up primarily of women." Her voice took on a condescending tone. "You, Steve, are a man. I wouldn't expect his blue eyes to affect you the way they affect me."

He lay back down on the sofa. "Really, I'm not saying I don't like his eyes." He angled a quick glance at her. "And now that I think about them—"

The pillow she threw landed on his chest.

"C.A., you hit me on my birthday."

"And you've got thirty-nine more whacks coming if you don't straighten up, S.B." She settled back in her chair. "Seriously, I'd like to give Devlin a chance, try to build him into a major character. If I think it's going in the wrong direction, I promise I'll eighty-six it."

"Okay, but I can feel my authority slipping right through my fingers."

"Your authority isn't slipping anywhere. I'm merely asking for your advice."

He sat up again and placed his beer can on the table next to the sofa. "If you feel that strongly about him, Cathy, go with that feeling, but remember, we have two hundred and sixty episodes to do each year. You're going to have to spread your interests around. Devlin can't be chief beneficiary of your time."

Cathy couldn't decide if Steve's remark was for her benefit as supervising producer of "SFL" or for her benefit as his new roommate. She hoped it was the latter.

She picked up her soda can and the empty beer can he had placed on the table. Seeing that she stood there, Steve looked up at her. By nature, she wasn't a flirt, but Steve seemed to bring out the worst—or was it the best?—in her. She gave him her sweetest smile.

"You're my boss, Steve...the chief beneficiary of my time."

As Cathy left the room she heard his musical, "Well, happy birthday to me."

Chapter Five

Sitting on the sofa, sharing the New York Times with Steve, Cathy leafed casually through the book review section. Then, even more casually, she asked, "Have you thought any more about Holly coming on board, Steve?"

He put the sports page down. "I thought you'd already decided on that. If she can make the job change we'll throw out the red carpet for her." He started to read again.

"She's arriving from L.A. tomorrow." Cathy half closed her eyes, waiting for his reaction. "I was sure you'd agree."

Down went the paper. "Sure?" He thought a moment. "Come to think about it, you are pretty sure of yourself, aren't you? Tell me, supervising producer, have you decided we should change networks, or any other little thing you think I should know about?"

"Not at the moment, sir."

"Not at the moment," he repeated. "You know, C.A., living with you is going to be an eye-opener."

"It was your idea," she reminded him.

His investigating look rested on the low-cut V of her loose-knit top. "In fact, it already is an eye-opener."

"Read your paper."

"I can't concentrate. I'm wondering what you're going to come up with next."

Cathy picked up the newspaper he had scattered on the floor, rolled up a few sheets, and tapped him on the head with it. "A woman likes to keep a man guessing."

"That's *two*, C.A."

"And only thirty-eight more to go." She started toward the kitchen with the papers. "Now what about this dinner you're supposed to be fixing?"

"What time is it?"

She glanced at the kitchen clock. "Six-forty."

"Oh, no! We're gonna miss it!" He jumped up and almost knocked her aside as he rushed through the kitchen door.

Recovering her balance, "Miss what?"

"Never mind. Are your hands clean?"

"Of course they are."

Condescension set in as he leaned his arms out across the counter top. "You know, newspaper does leave icky black print on your fingers."

"Well, excuse me. I'll wash them immediately."

"Good, then get the chicken from the fridge and wash the little devil out real good."

She tried to do so, but he fought her for space at the refrigerator door as he reached into the vegetable compartment for the celery.

"If I'm in your way, I'm sorry," she said apologetically.

"That's all right."

Taking the chicken to the sink, Cathy kept one eye on him as he quickly chopped celery into small pieces and quartered two onions and then reached into a cabinet for a covered casserole dish.

"What do you want me to do with the giblets, Steve?"

"Save the heart and wrap the rest in foil and toss them."

"What do you do with the heart?" she asked, somewhat confused.

"We make a wish on it...what else?"

She sighed deeply. "You do that with the wishbone, Chef Bronsky."

His sigh was even deeper. "Then, I ask you, what's the point in your keeping it? Dump it, too."

"How do you dry this chicken?"

"You just do this." He took the bird from her and shook it until she thought its wings would drop off.

Then he sprinkled the insides with salt, pepper and marjoram, stuffed the onions and celery in its cavity, and added more seasoning on the outside. A cup of water in the casserole dish and then he covered it.

"Now, birdie, into the oven at three twenty-five for two-and-a-half hours and you'll be tender and golden brown." He looked over at Cathy smugly. "And no basting, my dear."

Her applause was minimal. "Talk about not knowing what a person's going to do next."

Steve checked the wall clock, "Good, we're ahead of schedule."

"What schedule?"

"While that fowl is making itself gorgeous for us, we're taking a little trip."

"Where are we going?"

"Trust me. Oh. . .take your purse, you may need some money."

After rushing Cathy out the door, Steve hailed several cabs before one stopped and then they were on their way to the southernmost tip of Manhattan—Battery Park.

After they hurtled through a chasm between tall buildings, a broad expanse of blue sky suddenly loomed up before them and Cathy saw a broad green strip of trees ahead.

The cab screeched to a halt and then Cathy noticed the driver's smile widen as he took the generous tip Steve gave him. "Thanks, friend, you and the missus have a nice evening."

"The missus?" Cathy repeated, once the taxi pulled away.

"New York cab drivers are very perceptive. That guy knew that a handsome man like me would have to be taken. C'mon," he ordered her as he guided her through the heart of the park.

Cathy felt herself being forced to trot alongside him as he pulled her by the hand and hurried her to the railing at the water's edge.

"This is as far south as you can get on Manhattan." He pointed to his right. "The Hudson River." Then he pointed to his left. "And over there is the East River, and out there in the bay is my lady of the lake."

Cathy looked out over the gray-green water, feeling a warm, salty breeze rush across her face; she looked out beyond a ferry passing a tug pulling a barge of freight cars, and there in the distance she saw the Statue of Liberty.

The blue sky above was strewn with curls of clouds drifting through the wide expanse of space, but dusk threatened to chase the sun from the sky. Looking to her right, to the land mass on the other side of the Hudson, she saw the thick cloud of sullen smoke that she assumed was industrial pollution.

"Jersey," was all Steve said, and then he took her hand and walked her to a concession stand, where he asked for two Cokes. "Pay the man," he ordered, walking back toward the railing.

"So much for chivalry!" she yelled at his back.

Turning toward her, he replied, "Whose birthday is this?"

Cathy paid the man and joined Steve at the railing.

"Brace yourself," he warned, looking up at the sky.

Cathy followed his gaze, looking to her right and then to her left, wondering just what it was he was looking at.

"No, over there, toward Jersey," he said quietly.

She angled her eyes upward as he did and watched as the sun slowly transmuted itself into an enormous orange sphere and eased itself behind the smoke above the Jersey shore. She felt Steve's arm move to her shoulder as the sun reddened and the vast arch of incarnadine sky looked as though it had burst into flame.

Perhaps it was the magnificence of the moment, the almost unreal color of the sky, that caused Cathy's thoughts to drift backward in time, to another evening when she had watched a sunset with another man—a young man, or had

Jed at eighteen still been a boy? she wondered—but that other sunset had taken place fourteen years ago, when she and Jed had sat along a riverbank in Wisconsin, watching the sun disappear behind the hills to the west of the little town they lived in.

She recalled how gentlemanly he had been, spreading his new brown leather car coat on the ground for her to sit on, how concerned he had been for her comfort, how different she had looked in her high school outfit: the pleated skirt, heavy sweater, her hair pulled back in a ponytail. She had been surprised when Jack E. Daugherty, ''Jed'' to his friends, the star of their school's basketball team, had invited her to the senior prom as his date. Even after so many years, Cathy could still see his face, still remember his voice as they sat there on the river bank.

''Catherine, are you comfortable?''

''Very,'' she told him, raising her knees and tucking her skirt closer around her legs.

''Just maybe''—he hesitated nervously—''I mean I think there might be a blanket in the car from a picnic I went to last week. I could get it.''

''No. . .no, Jed. This is just fine.'' She lowered her knees, angled them gracefully, and brushed a leaf from his leather jacket. ''I can't stay long. My father expects me home early.''

''Catherine, what is it with that old man of yours? He treats you like you're still a little girl.''

''He says seventeen isn't all that grown-up. . .says that it's a dangerous age for a girl. Not a child and not yet a woman.''

He slipped down on the grass next to her, and ran his fingers through his thick brown hair.

As he did, Cathy watched him, perusing his handsome face, his wide jaw, the cleft chin, and again she really couldn't believe that he had asked *her* to go to the prom. After all, she told herself, he was so popular at school, particularly with the girls, and they had filled her ears with stories of their romantic interludes with him. A date with Jack E. Daugherty was like a certificate of entry into a special sisterhood. A girl he had dated was definitely *in*. And Cathy wanted so much to be *in* with that group, with those girls who had their special secrets, their special jokes, always laughing and seeming to be on top of everything. She wanted to laugh more, but to her father, too much gaiety was a sin.

"Catherine—"

"Yes, Jed?"

"You're a pretty girl, did you know that?"

Without wanting to, she blushed. "No, I'm not...not like the other girls at school."

"You're different," he agreed. "More serious."

"I can't help that. It's just the way I am, I guess."

"That's good. It sets you apart."

"But I don't want to be set apart, Jed. It's a lonely feeling," she admitted honestly.

Then she glanced at him. The evening breeze off the river swept against his brown mane, making him look like a young lion to her, a healthy and vibrant young animal who had the heart and the courage to do whatever he wanted to do, to go wherever he wanted to go, to take whatever he wanted to take.

"Jed," she asked quietly, "why did you invite me to the prom tomorrow night?"

"Because you're pretty, and we never have been out together." He ran his finger across the shoulder seam of her sweater. "And there's not that much time left, Catherine. I mean, when we graduate, that's it."

That's it. The words resounded in her ears.

And now that high school was nearing its end for her, Cathy felt as though an important chapter in her life was closing, a chapter filled with memories of watching Jed speed across the gym floor, seeing him leap high with the grace of a lynx to score for the home team, memories of watching his special swagger through the hallways at school—never alone, but always with girls hanging on to him adoringly, and each time she saw him touch them, even casually, she would pretend he was touching her. And now, out of the blue, he had chosen to be with her.

"I guess you're right, Jed. When we graduate we'll probably never see each other again, will we?"

"I'll still be here all summer."

"But after that?"

"Never say never, Catherine. Life is funny. You don't know what's going to happen until it actually happens." He ran his fingers down the arm of her sweater. Reaching her hand, he held it between his. "You have beautiful hands."

The very touch of him sent a rush of excitement up her arm, and when Jed began to move his palm lightly over her hand the excitement blossomed into a wondrous thrill that spread throughout her entire body.

"Can I kiss you?" he asked softly.

Her smile gave him his answer, and then his strong boy-ish face came close to hers, and for the first time she saw the slight blue tinge in his gray eyes, eyes that burned with an emotion that seemed too much for him to bear.

She felt his hand under her chin; then his lips touched hers, gently, with great tenderness. The warmth of his mouth and the fire in his eyes ignited the skin on her face, and then the flame seared her entire being.

Interrupting his kiss, he whispered, ''Put your arms around me, Catherine...please?''

Her eyes still closed, Cathy obeyed, guiding her youthful arms across his broad shoulders and around his strong neck. As she did, she felt him gently lower her onto the jacket under her and suddenly her nostrils were filled with the clean, pungent smell of leather, an almost intoxicating aroma.

And then she felt a nervousness in his mouth as his kiss began in earnest. At first she was startled by the fierce grinding of his mouth on hers, by his exploring hands, but as her young body reacted to the fire he had started deep within her, she relaxed and began to welcome the totally new feelings she discovered were a part of her, feelings that grew wilder, that were powerful, dizzying.

''Cathy!''

Her eyes shot open as Steve's arm shook her gently.

''You looked like you were miles away,'' he said, amused by the startled look in her eyes.

She blinked a few times. ''Miles and years away, Steve.''

Looking up at the sky again, Cathy watched as the clouds in the west became banks of crimson sided by hues of blue and purple; and then the violent colors slowly dissipated, leaving only the jeweled lights of the Palisades to welcome oncoming night.

"Man," Steve said huskily, looking across the river, "that gets to me every time."

Cathy quickly erased all thoughts of the past from her consciousness and just enjoyed the look on Steve's face, enjoyed the sensitivity she knew was such an important part of his nature.

"Well, C.A., what did you think of that?"

"That's quite a show your sunset puts on here."

Again his arm went around her shoulder, and she felt herself being drawn to him. "The show's so much better when you watch it with someone special."

"Listen, Bronsky, your chicken is only going to be a memory if we don't get back and watch it."

"Is that all you ever think about...eating? It's a wonder you're not overweight." He made a point of sizing her up. "Humph! I don't know how you do it."

Back at the house, the rooms were filled with the pleasant aroma of baked chicken, and when Steve deserted her for the kitchen, Cathy's eyes set on the wrapped package he had told her was her gift to him.

"I'm going to clean up, Steve. Need any help?"

"If you think I'm going to let you screw up my birthday dinner, lady, think again. Go ahead...and prepare your palate for a feast." His head appeared in the kitchen door. "You've got about a half hour...no longer or everything will be ruined."

Knowing that Steve was busy in the kitchen, Cathy didn't bother to close her bedroom door as she undressed and showered, telling herself that she should be concentrating on "SFL" but instead, she was looking forward to Steve's birthday party—cake, present, and all—as though it were the most important social event of the season. And after all, she had every right to enjoy being with him; they were just friends, nothing more. At least, that was what she told herself.

Powdered and perfumed, she began to move hangers to and fro, trying to decide what to wear. "Too dressy...too blah." She decided on a crimson outfit, not overly concerned with the sheerness of the bodice. "He liked the sunset...he'll like this dress," she told herself as she brushed her hair, leaving it flowing loosely, as he liked it.

Once downstairs, Cathy expected to find Steve running back and forth as she usually did at the eleventh hour when she had guests over for dinner, but instead she found him casually sitting in an easy chair, sipping on a cocktail; and somehow he had found time to change into a fresh white short-sleeved shirt that highlighted the tan of his muscular arms.

"Well, well." His eyes widened in appreciation. "If Ted could see you now, you'd have him eating out of the palm of your hand."

"Not bad for a middle-aged prude, huh?"

"You're not going to let me forget that, are you C.A.?"

"Not on your life, S.B."

"Maybe a cocktail will help you forget."

"I don't think so, Steve. Thanks anyway." Cathy took a whiff. "Umm...something does smell good. Broccoli?"

"Right. Hungry?"

"Starved."

"Well then, if madam will do me the honor"—he held out his arm—"dinner is served."

All through dinner, Steve tried to direct the conversation to finding out more about Cathy, why she had never married, and why, as she told him, there was no special man in her life waiting for her in California. At one point, it seemed to her, he was again interested in why she had left Wisconsin to go live with her aunt in Hollywood.

"Enough about me," she said abruptly. "What about you? Why aren't you married?" She wiped her lips with her napkin. "Never mind. I know why. You're so perfect that you just haven't been able to find a woman good enough for you. Or maybe it's just that you can't stand children."

She smiled at what she thought was light banter, only to see that rare dark mood settle in his face.

Then, softly, he answered, "None of the above." He grabbed a few dishes and made for the kitchen.

For a moment Cathy just remained seated, wondering what she had said to cause the instantaneous change in him. Then she, too, began carrying dishes into the kitchen.

"Steve, I'll take care of these. Remember, you're the birthday boy," she told him trying to bring the smile back to his face.

"Let's both cart. It'll be quicker, and I'm dying to see what you bought me."

"So am I," she added.

With the dishes rinsed, he convinced her that they wouldn't run away and they would be there for her to finish the next day. Then, after pouring them both a Calvados, he put on a tape. He lowered the volume and sat on the sofa. "Well, when are you going to give me my birthday present?" Looking at his watch, he declared, "In two hours I'll be forty and a day."

"Okay," she said, getting up from her chair to hand him the package. "The suspense is killing me."

"It's lovely...you shouldn't have," he teased.

"It was nothing, really. But the minute I saw it, I knew it was you." Her arm gestured toward him flamboyantly.

"Should I try to save the paper?"

"Open it! I want to see what I bought you."

Steve tore into the package with a frenzy, opened the lid of the large box, and moaned, "Ah...just what I need."

Cathy stretched her neck, trying to see what it was that impressed him so, but he deliberately held the contents from her view.

"Are you going to show me *my* gift to you, or not?" she asked, trying to sound serious.

"Here." He handed her the closed box. "See for yourself."

Removing the cover, she pushed the white tissue paper aside, finding only a small plastic-wrapped package, which she lifted from the box.

"Fruit of the Loom!" she shrieked, holding the package of three pairs of brown undershorts.

He smiled charmingly. "You really are thoughtful. You think of everything. They'll go nicely with my robe."

Cathy threw the package back into the oversized box, carried it to the sofa, and tossed it down next to him. "It's a good thing today's your birthday, or—"

"Or what?"

The blare of Guy Lombardo's music hit her ears. "Would you please change that tape? Somehow, 'Auld Lang Syne' in the heat of August makes me feel like I'm in a time warp...in fact, *you* make me feel like I'm in a time warp."

He switched to an FM station and pleasant background music flowed from the speakers.

"Better?"

"Much."

"Are you ready to serve my birthday cake?"

"Do you have forty candles?"

"There's one on it already. That says it all, don't you think?"

"It doesn't say what I'm thinking," she teased him.

Cathy went into the dining room, to the buffet on which he had placed the bakery box. She opened the lid and there on the cake, scrawled in blue icing, she read *Happy Birthday S.B.—Love, C.A.*

The moisture that tickled her eyelids was quickly wiped away; she was glad he wasn't in the room with her. He was a nut, she told herself, but a nice nut.

Carefully she placed the cake on the platter he had set out. Then she lit the single candle and called to him.

"Are you coming in here, or do you expect me to carry this monster out there?"

Standing at the doorway he said, "What would I do with a supervising producer who had a hernia?"

That soft smile of his again; that feeling of excitement rippling across her chest. "Can't you be serious even for a minute? This is an important moment. You have to make a wish and blow out the candles"—she eyed the lone flame—"the candle."

"Right."

He looked at the candle, then looked at her, back at the candle, and to her again, his face tortured as though he were making a difficult decision.

"Bronsky, will you please blow out the candle! It's going to drip all over your cake."

"Our cake," he corrected. Puffing his cheeks and inhaling as though all forty were there, he blew it out. "I'd tell you what I wish, but I don't want to goof it up."

Cathy handed him the cake knife and said, "You probably wished for a nude showgirl to pop out of the cake."

"What could I possibly do with a nude showgirl...and you?" he asked suggestively.

"Just cut the cake."

He started to cut, but stopped. "Say, don't I get another wish when I cut this?"

"Of course."

The way his brow furrowed before he smiled made it look as though he were enjoying some special secret.

With cake cut and eased onto plates, they went back into the living room and began to eat.

"You know, Cathy, this has been one of my better birthdays," he said sincerely.

She nestled back in her chair. "I'm glad, Steve...I really am. The whole weekend's been fun, but tomorrow's going to be another story."

"Not to worry. That's a good group we've got at the studio, and when they see that I've accepted you, they will, too."

"And have you really?" she asked quietly.

"Have I what?"

"Accepted the fact that it was necessary for me to come on the scene."

"I'm not a person who lies to himself, Cathy. I knew there were problems long before the big boys upstairs knew it."

She hesitated, but then decided to pursue. "Why didn't you do something about it? Why did you wait until the ratings fell through the floor? What did happen?"

Steve's fingers eased slowly across his forehead; his eyes sought hers. When they met, Cathy saw the indecision in them. Then, his voice sounded, low, painful. "An accident...a divorce. I just—" He stopped.

Cathy watched as his lips moved ever so slightly, as though he were trying to speak but couldn't; then she saw the reserve, the withdrawal cloud his eyes over. He got up, took her plate and went into the kitchen. She started to follow, but the sudden sound of the front door buzzer startled her.

"Want me to get it?" she called to him.

"Okay, but see who it is first."

Forgetting that she was barefoot, she went to the door and looked through the peephole, not seeing anyone until she glanced downward to see the face of a young boy. Moving the slide bolt, she unlocked the door and pulled it open.

The boy couldn't have been more than twelve or thirteen, she guessed. He was neatly dressed and had a small gift in his hand. Seeming surprised at seeing Cathy, he spoke quietly. "Is my dad here?"

Chapter Six

How little I really know about Steve!

That was Cathy's first thought as she looked down at the boy, quickly taking in his features—the same shine in his eyes, the same dark brown hair, although the boy's hair lacked Steve's carefree waviness.

"Come in...please," she said awkwardly, suddenly remembering she was barefoot. "Steve...your father is here...uh—"

"Robert," he said quickly, darting past her. "Dad! It's me!"

"Robbie?" Steve's voice registered the same surprise she had experienced. "What's wrong? What're you doing here? It's after eleven. Where's your mother?"

Give the boy a chance to say something, Cathy thought, still standing in the foyer, wondering if she should just saunter casually back to the living room.

"She took Franklin to the airport. Said she'd be back in time for me to bring you your birthday present but she wasn't so I brought it myself."

"How'd you get here?"

"I walked."

"You walked! Alone, from Sutton Place?"

"Sure. I just followed Fifth Avenue down to the square."

"Oh my God!" Steve moaned as Cathy decided to join them, hurrying to retrieve her shoes. "Robbie, why didn't you phone me? I'd have come to get you."

"I did, Dad, but you didn't answer."

Steve thought a moment. Then he said, "Does Hilda know you came here?"

The boy shuffled his feet uneasily and looked down. "No. She wouldn't have let me."

Steve rushed to the study. "Knowing Hilda, I'll bet she's got the police combing the streets already."

Cathy sat down and tried to be inconspicuous. She smiled weakly when Robbie looked her way, feeling uneasy when he didn't return her smile, but then her attention was diverted to Steve's voice coming from the study.

"No, Hilda...stop crying...he's fine. I'll get him home in just a little while. Is Mrs. Rimbaud there? Not yet? Well, maybe you should have the police looking for her! No, Hilda, I didn't mean that. Hilda, will you please calm down. We'll be there shortly."

When Steve did come back into the living room, Cathy could see that he was still upset.

"Robbie, you just about gave Hilda a nervous breakdown. You know how she gets. And she found your wallet on your dresser, so she knew you didn't have money on you. Why didn't you at least take a cab here?" Then, before the boy could answer, he exclaimed, "Cathy, do you know what this kid just did...do you know?"

Feeling very uncomfortable for the boy, she shook her head.

"He just walked half the length of Manhattan at night in the damn dark." In exasperation, Steve let his body fall on the sofa.

Still squirming, his son informed him, "It's not dark on Fifth Avenue, Dad. Not all the way."

Unfortunately, Steve saw the smile on Cathy's face. His glare erased it immediately.

Holding his little package behind him, Robbie ran his finger along the arm of the sofa. "I thought you'd be glad to see me, Dad," he mumbled.

For the second time that evening, Cathy's eyes moistened when Steve grabbed the boy in his arms and hugged him tightly.

"Ah, Robbie, I am glad...you know I am, but you scared the hell out of me. What if something had happened to you, too?"

Cathy didn't understand the *you, too*, but from the desperate look on Steve's face, she wasn't sure she wanted to.

He held the boy by the shoulders, looked him squarely in the face. "You know your mother's going to have a fit when she learns about this. You won't see TV for a year. And you know who she's going to blame, don't you?" Then, looking at Robbie's missing eyetooth, he asked, "Where'd you lose that?"

"Football," he answered proudly.

"Oh, God, she'll nail me for that, too." Starting to calm down, Steve glanced over at Cathy. "Excuse me, Cathy...I'd like you to meet my son, Robbie. Robbie, this is Cathy Arensen. We work together."

Robbie crossed the room and extended his hand. "Pleased to meet you, Mrs. Arensen." He just assumed all grown-ups were married.

"Miss Arensen, Robbie, but why don't you call me Cathy."

He looked over at his father. Steve nodded approval.

"Pleased to meet you, Cathy." Then he sat next to his father on the sofa. "Don't you want your present, Dad?"

"You bet I do." Taking the offered, somewhat childishly wrapped little package, Steve said, "Hey did you wrap this yourself? That's neat."

Satisfaction spread over his son's face.

The package opened, Steve pulled out a beaded Indian belt, not quite perfectly made, but a gift he would cherish the rest of his life. "Robbie, this is just super!"

"I made it, Dad," he bragged. "From a kit I got in a crafts shop in Palm Beach, and I paid for it myself. I worked on it all summer."

"Has your mother seen this?" Steve asked, his voice still filled with admiration.

"Not finished. I wanted to surprise her, too."

"Well, then, we'll do just that." He slipped the prized beaded belt through the loops of his slacks. Then, standing up for all to admire, he said, "Ever seen anything like this before, Cathy?"

"Never. Robbie, you do beautiful work."

"It's not hard, it just takes a lot of patience."

Then, Cathy had an idea. "Robbie, how would you like a piece of birthday cake?"

"And some milk," Steve added.

Robbie's little face looked anguished. "Did you guys have a birthday party?" he asked disappointedly, feeling he'd been left out.

Cathy saw the pained look that crossed Steve's face.

"Not really a party, Robbie," he explained. "I wouldn't have had a real birthday party without you, would I?" He got up and placed a hand on the boy's shoulder. "C'mon, let's get a glass of milk to go with that cake and then it's home and bed for you, young man."

When they started off toward the kitchen, Cathy went into the dining room and cut a piece of cake, being careful not to slice through the word *love*. She was about to take it to the living room, but then decided Robbie would be more comfortable eating it at the table, rather than having to juggle the dish on his lap. "In here okay, Robbie?" she called.

"Sure...wow, look at that." Cathy had cut him an end piece that was covered on two sides with the rich, creamy icing.

While Robbie wolfed down the cake and milk, Cathy put together the pieces of the conversation between father and son. From the various cues, she gathered that Steve's ex-wife had remarried—to a Franklin Rimbaud—that Robbie and his mother had spent the summer in Palm Beach, and that the boy would be going to a New York prep school in the fall. The one thing she still had no inkling about was Steven's saying *you, too* earlier in the evening.

"Okay, Robbie, it's time to face the music," Steve said solemnly.

The boy looked up at Cathy. "You're gonna come with us, aren't you?"

The extra, thin slice of cake she had provided had endeared her to him.

"Oh, I don't think so, Robbie."

"Why don't you?" Steve asked. "I'd like you to meet Meredith." His eyes told her that he was serious, that there was some reason he did want her to meet his ex-wife, although Cathy didn't see how the meeting could possibly be a pleasant one, considering the circumstances and the time of night.

"Come on, Cathy," Robbie pleaded. "It'll sure make it easier on my dad and me if you're there."

"So that's it. You both want me there for protection."

Robbie sidled next to his father and put his little arm around Steve's waist. "There are some things only a woman can accomplish, Cathy."

"Oh, brother!" Cathy murmured. "I wonder where you got that line from." A quick smile at Steve. "Okay, you two, let me get my purse."

Going upstairs, she couldn't help overhearing Robbie say, "She's pretty, Dad, and she's a miss, too."

The cab ride to Sutton Place on Manhattan's East Side was too brief as far as Cathy was concerned. She wasn't looking forward to meeting Meredith Rimbaud, and she was certain Mrs. Rimbaud couldn't possibly be looking forward to meeting her, but her two male companions in the taxi were both excellent con artists.

The doorman outside the fashionable apartment building opened the cab door and welcomed Steve like an old friend and then escorted the little group into the plush lobby.

The elevator ride was a quiet one, each of the three mentally imagining what *Mother* was going to say. They needn't have worried, though, since Hilda, the maid, told them upon arriving that Mrs. Rimbaud had still not returned from the airport.

Cathy glanced around the entry hall and then followed Steve and Robbie into a large, almost empty room that had a two-storey ceiling. The parquet floor was glossy. Above the two heavily carved doors on either side of the far wall, and covering the entire wall, was a mural of the map of the world; a gold line starting at New York connected various cities around the world and then wound up back at New York. Underneath the imposing mural, in gold, were the words *The Grand Tour of Louise and Meredith Anderman.*

"Odd-looking room, isn't it?" Steve said. "Used as a dance floor for small parties." He pointed up to a balcony built into the wall behind her. "Small combos sit up there."

Just then, Cathy heard the front door open. Turning, she saw an elegantly dressed woman with dark hair walk gracefully through the entry hall.

"Steven?" She gave a quick glance at Cathy and then said, "Robert, why aren't you in bed? Where is Hilda?" Her voice was soft and cultured.

"Considering the hour," Steve said, "I told Hilda to go to bed."

Again the dark-haired woman looked at Cathy. Then she turned toward Steve, her blue eyes requesting an explanation.

"Meredith, I'd like you to meet Catherine Arensen, my supervising producer. Cathy, Robbie's mother, Meredith Rimbaud."

"Mrs. Rimbaud," Cathy said politely.

The woman's steely blue eyes examined Cathy quickly.

"Really, Steven, it is rather late for a social call, and you know how I detest surprises."

"Meredith, Robbie—"

"Robert," she interrupted, "are you all right?"

"He's fine," Steve told her. "He just wanted to bring me my birthday present."

"Oh, that." The woman's indifference was all too obvious.

An awkward silence hung over the room for a moment. Finally Steve spoke up. "Okay, sport, let's hit it." He put his hand on Robbie's shoulders and led him toward the door on the left.

Seeing his mother's back to him, Robbie held up his hand, making a circle with his thumb and index finger, forming an even stronger bond between him and his "cake lady."

Unfortunately, Meredith turned toward him in time to see his little gesture, which he immediately discontinued. She glared back at Cathy, only to see the smile on her face.

"Steven, I'll be along in a moment. We can't just leave Miss Arensen standing here, can we?" She then extended her arm gracefully to the door on the right and Cathy followed her into a beautifully appointed salon.

"I don't know what kind of horror story Steven is going to tell me, but as long as Robert is safe, that's all that matters."

Cathy watched as Mrs. Rimbaud slipped off her jacket and laid it across the back of a tall wing chair.

"Would you like some Chambord, Miss Arensen? Or perhaps you'd care for something stronger.

"Chambord is fine, thank you."

Cathy watched as the woman reached for the small orb-shaped bottle trimmed in gold with a gold crown at its top. With delicate fingers she removed the little crown and half-filled two crystal liqueur glasses. Replacing its top, she held the orb in her slender hand and Cathy became aware of the intense regalness of the woman.

"Have you known Steven long?" she asked in her well-modulated voice.

"No, I only arrived from California last Friday." She sipped the liqueur, tasting the flavor of black raspberries and the suggestion of honey.

"And already he has you working day and night." Again those inspecting blue eyes. "Please sit down and make yourself comfortable. I want to check on Robert. Forgive me for leaving you alone. We won't be long."

She put her glass down and started to leave the room, but then she suddenly stopped and turned toward Cathy. "Miss Arensen, if you find yourself terribly attracted to Steven, don't be surprised. He has a certain charm about him. . .at first. I know." Her eyes lowered momentarily, as though she was deciding whether or not to continue. Then, she did.

"At one time I was attracted to him, but he's an extremely difficult man to live with. I don't believe many women would be able to cope with his. . .idiosyncrasies." She smiled, slightly, and left the room.

Alone in the poshly furnished drawing room, Cathy analyzed the woman who had just left. There was a certain coolness about her, or was it just inbred reserve? She was not a woman Cathy would choose for a friend.

Cathy glanced at her wristwatch. Midnight had come and gone, and she started to dread hearing her clock radio go off in the morning.

Her thoughts returned to Steve's ex-wife and to Steve. She found it difficult to think of them as a pair. Her reserve was the antithesis of his fun-loving sense of humor, but then Cathy had already decided that sometimes Steve used his wit to cover up some sense of pain he was harboring. She wondered how long they had been married. Robbie was thirteen, she had learned, the same age as—no, she had promised herself she would never think about that. She forced herself to consider how long ago they must have been married. At least fourteen years, she estimated.

Another sip of Chambord, and then she noticed the collection of Wedgwood birds arranged in an open cabinet near the grand piano. Even in the dim light, the small solid blocks of fine crystal magically created a shimmering rainbow of colors, each sculpture— "Sorry to have deserted you, Cathy," Steve apologized, drawing her attention from the little Wedgewood pieces. "Robbie's all set, and I'd better get you home, too."

"Yes, tomorrow is a work day," Cathy said, simply to have something to say.

"Do you really enjoy your work, Miss Arensen? I would think being involved with those soap operas day after day would be boring after a while."

Cathy smiled pleasantly. "Odd that you should think that, Mrs. Rimbaud. I find my work and my colleagues quite exciting."

Enjoying the perturbed look on his ex-wife's face, Steve suggested they leave.

The good-byes were curt, and during the cab ride back to the Village, Steve explained why the evening had gone so awry for everybody. Meredith had promised she would take Robbie to his father's to give him his gift, but when her husband's plane was late in departing, she had decided to wait with him instead.

"Aren't you glad you have a birthday just once a year?" Cathy joked as Steve locked the door behind them.

"You don't have to be nice to me anymore, C.A. It's after midnight."

"Steve, I'm too tired to be mean to anyone right now. All I want to do is to get to bed. I don't know about you, but I'm exhausted, physically and mentally."

She started up the stairs, but his voice followed her.

"What did you think of Meredith?"

"She's a beautiful woman."

"Yes," he said thoughtfully, "she is, isn't she?"

Was it regret she heard in his voice? she wondered, and then she assumed the slight ache she felt in her chest was fatigue. Yes, she assured herself, it could only be fatigue. What else?

"Good night, Steve."

"Night, Cathy. Sleep well, and thanks for being so nice to Robbie. You may just wind up being his first love, and I can't say as though I'd blame him. You're a woman any man could fall in love with...very easily."

Don't say things like that, she wanted to yell, *it just confuses me.* Instead, she just smiled and went to her bedroom.

Cathy had no trouble falling asleep, but something made her sleep restless. With half-opened eyes she peered out into the hallway and saw the weak shaft of light that she knew came from Steve's room. A quick glance at her digital clock told her it was almost two in the morning. Wondering why he wasn't sleeping, she sat up in bed. Was something wrong? She got up and put on her robe. Barefoot, she took slow steps on the carpeted hallway toward his room.

Glancing in, she saw him sitting in a chair by the window, smoking a cigarette. The ashtray on the window ledge was half full of discarded butts. His brown robe and disheveled bed suggested that he had tried to sleep but was unable to.

"Steve," she said softly, "are you all right?"

Without looking at her, he angled his head toward the door. "I'm fine. I didn't mean to wake you. Please...go back to bed." His voice was colorless, emotionless.

She walked to the bottom of the bed and sat down near him. "You don't look fine to me. Can't sleep?"

"No." Another puff. "One of those nights, I guess."

"Want me to fix you some warm milk?"

"No, no...thanks, anyway."

"Well, you just can't sit there all night and smoke yourself to death."

Suddenly his voice became harsh. "It hasn't killed me yet!"

Cathy supposed that he had spent many a night like this, and immediately she wondered if that was why he hadn't been able to give his work the creative time it needed so desperately.

"Insomnia?"

"More like a guilt trip," he said, as though disgusted with himself.

"Steve, half the marriages in this country don't make it. That's no reason for a self-imposed guilt complex."

"The divorce has nothing to do with it."

He got up abruptly, grabbed the ashtray, and walked to the bathroom, not with his usual graceful steps, but with a plodding gait that made the strong muscles in his long legs bulge with every step.

"Why don't you go back to bed?" he said roughly when he came back.

"If you shut me out, Steve, I can't help you...and I really want to help."

"It's too late for help. The damage has already been done."

"Steve, there's nothing that can't—"

"That's talk...just talk!" His face became a grimace that frightened her. "And words won't bring him back."

He stormed to his dresser, opened a drawer, slammed it shut, and opened another, taking a fresh pack of cigarettes out and tearing the top open. He lit one, threw the lighter down on the dresser, and then leaned forward, arms outstretched, his back to her.

Looking over at him as he hunched over the dresser, she could see his mirrored reflection and knew that he was hurting; his hurt made her suffer, too.

"Steve," she began cautiously, "won't bring *who* back?"

He turned, his face crimson. The hand holding his cigarette lifted into the air. Pointing directly at her, he snarled, "You have a sadistic streak in you. You won't be satisfied until you hear all the gory details, will you?"

The hate in his voice rushed at her like the cold wind before a winter storm. She felt her lip quiver, felt her skin tingle with fear. Her first thought was to run from the room, to leave him alone with his suffering, but something else— she wasn't sure what—anchored her to his bed. Her fingers bunched up the thrown-back sheet as she lifted her glistening eyes to his.

"I didn't mean to pry, Steve. I only wanted to try to help."

When he saw the tear roll down her cheek, his face softened; he looked helpless, as though he felt of no value to himself or to anyone else. Slowly he snuffed out his cigarette and rubbed his forehead with his fingers.

"Cathy, I'm sorry."

Sitting next to her on the bed, he enclosed her in his arms. And now her tears came, washing away the fear and the hurt he had heaped on her. She thrust the palm of her hand against his chest for support as he held her closely, rocking her gently, feeling as though her tears were washing away some of his pain.

"There, there," he said soothingly. "I hate women who cry."

Her muffled voice answered, "And I hate men who are too stubborn to share their problems."

Looking down at her in mock disbelief, he asked, "Stubborn? Me?"

"You!"

"Well, maybe a little," he conceded, forcing a weak smile.

She bolted upright. "And you don't have the market on suffering, Steve. Everyone's had problems."

"I've told myself that a hundred times, Cathy, but it doesn't seem to help."

"I'm not sure you really want help."

He looked at her quizzically. "What's that supposed to mean?" Then, before she could answer, he was at the dresser lighting another cigarette.

"I'm no psychiatrist, Steve, but I've known people who've used suffering to hold on to someone or something they've lost."

He placed the ashtray on the night table and lay on the bed, his back arched against the headboard, careful to make sure his short robe covered his thighs. He took a deep puff, looking at her with thoughtful eyes, and then he extended his left arm.

"C'mere."

With no hesitation, Cathy slid up next to him on the bed and let him pull her toward his body. Firmly held, she snuggled close, resting her head on his chest, one hand slipping inside his opened robe.

Her palm vibrated with each heartbeat she felt thump against his warm flesh; her nervous fingers curved over the solid muscle of his chest while her thumb strayed across the soft hair under her hand.

Slowly he began, "Meredith and I had two boys, Cathy. Robbie, thirteen, and little Stevie who was only nine years old. Last summer..."—he swallowed hard and then continued—"I took them to Rockaway Beach. Meredith and her mother had gone shopping. There we were, the three of us, three little boys playing pirate on the beach. I was the treasure and they were burying me in the sand. I moaned and begged for mercy. They laughed and sand flew everywhere. Robbie put this huge pail over my head so the sand wouldn't get in my eyes. I could feel the sand being piled on me, but then it seemed that the laughter had died down."

He put out his cigarette, and then she felt his other arm hold her also.

"I shook the pail off my head and looked around. Robbie was still heaping sand on top of me, but little Stevie was nowhere in sight. He had gone into the water, Robbie said.''

Cathy felt his arms tighten about her shoulder until it hurt.

''I looked down the beach and saw some men running into the water. I got loose from the sand and ran down, too, looking for some sign of Stevie along the water's edge. There was none. I called his name again and again, wanting to believe he was still somewhere on the beach, and then I looked out into the water. No sign of him, but some men were swimming in one direction, so I jumped in and began swimming their way.''

Under her hand, Cathy could feel his chest beginning to heave, his heartbeat quicken.

''The strong undertow pulled at my body. God, it was strong, and suddenly I knew it would be impossible for a little boy to fight it. By then a lifeguard was circling in his boat, trying to find something to go after...but, nothing. He was just gone, Cathy. One minute he was playing happily on the beach, and the next Stevie was gone.''

His body was now literally shaking under her hand; the skin that had been warm under her palm had become hot.

''I should have watched him more carefully, Cathy. I should have *watched* over him more carefully!'' he cried out, cursing himself.

And then Cathy felt the moisture that eased onto her forehead, knowing it was his tears. She didn't dare look up at him—she knew she would cry, too.

''Steve,'' she whispered, as she stroked his chest soothingly, ''it was an accident. There was nothing you could have done. While Stevie was with you, I'm sure he was loved more than most children could ever hope to be.''

Cathy could feel him shaking more violently and she thought that perhaps this was the first time he had ever really given vent to his inner agony. Raising herself higher on the bed, she pulled him toward her, resting his head on her breast, one arm around him. With her other hand, she switched off the lamp next to her and then placed both her arms about him.

"It's been a nightmare, Cathy...a damned nightmare," he mumbled, his tearful face resting deeply on her bosom.

"I know Steve...I know. It's hard to lose someone we love. Nothing in life prepares you for it but somehow we get through it, don't we?"

As Steve lay there in the warmth of Cathy's embrace, she felt a calmness slowly return to the stiffened muscles of his back. She rubbed harder, trying to comfort him, trying to let him know he wasn't alone in his anguish, that she was there with him. Her fingers swept across his cheek; she leaned toward him and kissed his head, not caring that his hands had begun a soothing caress of her body. All that mattered to her was that he was beginning to relax. His face nuzzled deeper into the low cut of her gown and she felt him pulling her closer to his warm body.

"Stay with me tonight, Cathy...please. Don't leave me...not tonight."

His pleading came slowly, a pleading she couldn't refuse.

Cathy had held few men in her arms since she had turned seventeen, and now in this moment as she held Steve, she knew for a certainty how little the other men had mattered to her. She closed her eyes and rested her chin on his head, basking in the warmth of his body close to hers, in the thrill of the feel of his strong back under her fingertips.

Again she kissed his soft waves. "I won't leave you," she said softly.

Slowly he raised his head from her breasts. The eyes that had laughed at her, had mocked her in fun, had joked with her—were now reddened and weary. "Promise?"

"Promise," she whispered back.

In the next moment Cathy felt his lips touch her throat; an electrifying sensation rushed across her bosom, creating havoc with each and every nerve end in her body. Then she felt his hot breath move slowly across her cheek, stopping occasionally to imprint a delicate kiss on her face— and then the taste of his breath as his lips lingered close to hers before gently settling, once, twice, and for a third time.

She watched as his face moved away from hers, and in his eyes she saw his question; she sighed in relief when she realized her heart had sent an answer to her own eyes—an answer that Steve was able to interpret correctly.

Rising from the bed, Steve switched off the lamp on his side, leaving the room bathed only in the light of the bright moon that filtered through the window panels. Watching his silhouette, Cathy saw him remove his robe and let it fall to the floor. Still watching, her heart beating more rapidly, she saw his arm reach up and push back the panel from the window, allowing the soft moonlight to flood the room.

At the window Steve was but a dark shadow, but when he walked to the bottom of the bed toward Cathy's side, the moonlight bathed his tanned body with golden light, igniting his eyes.

Moving closer to her, he extended his hands. Taking them, she felt him pulling her from the bed with great gentleness. And then, as he glanced at her shoulders, he slipped the robe from her, tenderly kissing each bare shoulder as his arms encircled her waist and pulled her up against his body.

Slowly her palms slid up his firm chest, her fingertips tingling at the feel of the soft swirls across his solid muscles. Lingering momentarily as if to memorize the touch of him, her hands then reached over his shoulders to the back of his strong neck and slid up into the wavy mass of soft brown hair. Guiding her fingers across his warm ears, she held his face between her trembling fingers and slowly pressed her lips to his. As his moan of delight filled her ears, she eased her tongue past his waiting lips.

Feeling his fingers take hold of the straps of her gown, Cathy lowered her arms, letting him free the straps from her shoulders, all the while prolonging the kiss that she wanted to last forever—forever and beyond eternity. Never wanting the moment to change, she longed to be swept away with the feel of him, longed for the touch of his hands on her body to remain with her always. Arching back, she let her silken gown slip to the carpet beneath them as her mouth rolled against his, as their tongues darted, pushed, tasted—their lips embedded ecstatically in each other's.

Her head dizzy with expectation, Cathy felt herself being lifted and gently set down on his huge bed. With closed eyes she felt the bed give way to the weight of his body next to hers, felt him adjust the pillow under her head, and then his hand rest on her breast, gently fingering its taut bud. At the crossing of his leg over hers, she realized the enormity of his desire for her, a desire that had already set fire to her own.

His one hand searching at her breast, she felt his other brush back wayward strands of her hair that had fallen forward. Again his lips brushed hers, softly and tenderly, and then he lowered his mouth to her heaving breasts to bring his warm moisture to calm the fire within them.

Cathy opened her eyes as she breathed deeply to make up for the moments when she could hardly breathe. The fire in her body raged as his kisses moved downward across her firm stomach—and further, even, as his lips and tongue began a dance of flaming desire that sent her brain reeling, that racked her body with the sweetest of spasms. Then, sensing that she was at the brink of ecstasy, Steve's lips moved upward once more, up to the hardened nipples that he caressed in turn with his eager mouth and tongue.

When Steve's face did come into Cathy's view, she saw it through the filter of the soft moonlight. It was the only face in the world that mattered to her, the only face she wanted to touch, to kiss. Her fingers fanned across his full lips, swept down onto his strong jawline and then moved up across his stubbled cheek, roaming about his ear and onto the small scar at his temple.

Her hand cupped his neck and she drew his face down to her, inviting his lips to caress hers once more. As their breath mingled she felt his strong, yet gentle, fingers continue the dance that his lips and tongue had begun at the soul of her desire only moments before. Reaching downward, she pressed him to her, half wanting to rush ahead, half wanting to prolong the sweet agony that tormented her entire being.

At the touch of her hand, Steve moaned with delight and eased his body onto hers as she guided the fullness of him into the warmth of her body. A soft gasp passed from her mouth into his as she felt his weight bear down on her, as he filled her. Her hands reaching around to his back, she

pulled him as close to her as she could, suffering the glo-
riously painful hardness of his body as her probing fingers
traced deep indentations along his back muscles and made
their way downward until they dug into the firm softness of
his warm flesh.

Her head rocked from side to side, but his mouth followed hard on hers as their movements became more
impetuous, as they flowed in unison to some wildly pri-
mitive rhythm that thundered in Cathy's ears. A shining
vortex began to spin in her closed eyes—silver, then gold,
then the brilliant crimson and blues of a recent sunset
splashed out at her. Desperately holding on to him with all
her strength, she suddenly arched upward as he shuddered
involuntarily again and again.

It was then that she heard her own voice cry out his name
as wave after wave of mind-shattering bliss mingled with
the abundant love he filled her with.

Time stopped momentarily for her, and then she felt as
though she were floating downward from an ecstatic obliv-
ion—floating, yet moving to the sound of a rhythmic beat.
As her sensitivities normalized, she realized it was the
pounding of Steve's heart against hers. Exhausted, she lay
there, her arms still about him in the quiet of the night,
feeling the beads of their perspiration mingle in their
closeness, feeling the same warmth inside as she felt
outside.

For minutes they rested that way, each one welcoming
the breaths that came easier. Then, holding her tightly to
his body, refusing to remove the still firm bond that united
them, Steve rolled onto his side and guided Cathy's head to
his shoulder.

Not a word passed between them; none was necessary as Steve's hand moved slowly across her arm and back until a peaceful sleep came to both of them.

Chapter Seven

The scribbled note taped to the night table lamp read: *No. 1. Do not turn over and go back to sleep. Go get coffee, dress, and come to work. P.S. Your name is Catherine Arensen and you are in my bed.*

Cathy had known she was in Steve's bed as soon as her eyes had opened and her own yellow drapes were replaced by his tan and gold ones. Quickly the entire crazy evening—and night—had flashed before her eyes. Even though she had found herself alone in his room, she had pulled the sheet up around her to cover her nakedness. For a moment, she had lain back on his pillow trying to recapture the face that had been so close to hers in the moonlight, trying to relive the feel of his body against hers.

Then she had bolted up, found her robe, and hurriedly slipped it on. She had had no regrets, no remorse, only a deep sense of complications entering her life, a life she had long ago decided would be devoid of such complications. And then she had found his note on the lamp.

"Nut!" she mumbled as she picked up her nightgown and went to her own bathroom.

There on the mirror over the washbasin was note number two: *I said to get coffee first!*

"Pushy, aren't you," she remarked and then turned the tub water on for her bath.

A half hour later, wrapped in her terry-cloth robe, Cathy walked into the kitchen to find two pieces of wheat toast in the toaster, ready to be pushed down. On the counter, butter and strawberry jam, and coffee maker ready and waiting for her.

Taped to the toaster—note number four. Immediately she wondered where she had missed number three. Then, reading: *In case you're wondering, there is no No. 3. Just wanted to make sure you were alert before using an electrical appliance. P.S. Please hurry. I miss you.*

"I miss you," she told him out loud, at the same moment experiencing a longing to be near him and a frightening warning signal of encroaching danger.

After putting the bread back in its package and the butter and jam in the refrigerator, Cathy poured herself a cup of black coffee and took it to her room while she got herself ready for work, all the while trying to sort out the conflicting emotions that filled her thinking.

Don't make a big deal out of last night, she told herself. Steve was upset. He needed somebody and you were there. It could have been anyone else. You're not going to let one night turn your life upside down.

She arranged her hair in a severe bun and picked out her most businesslike suit to wear, continuing to gird herself with reasons not to recognize the tenderness and honesty of Steve's feelings for her, convincing herself that he had made love to her to assuage the pain of his own unhappiness, convincing herself that she was just setting herself up for another *good-bye*.

Then she hit on the argument that had always proved a sure-fire reason for her to avoid emotional commitments. *You were burned once, Catherine Arensen,* she reminded herself. *Are you going to let it happen again?*

"No!" came the answer as she picked up her handbag and attaché case and left for the studio.

It was after ten o'clock when she walked into the large gray rehearsal room, its blank walls holding only a bulletin board with assorted announcements, messages and notices of interest to the cast of "SFL."

Along one side were filing cabinets and storage boxes, old folding chairs, and a large wooden cabinet riddled with pigeonholes labeled with the names of the cast and stuffed with fan mail.

On the other side of the rather depressing room was a table holding a coffee machine and a box of doughnuts. At the long table running through the middle of the room, she saw one of the directors and some cast members going over their scripts, foam cups in their hands.

Steve was sitting with them, but it was a moment before he saw Cathy come in the door. Immediately he left the group and walked over to her. He kept his voice subdued.

"Good morning." His eyes caressed her. "Sleep well?"

Cathy decided he had seen the indecision in her eyes, because she noticed the questioning look that settled in his.

"Why did you let me sleep so late, Steve? I've already missed two meetings."

She hoped he would construe her guarded look as one of concern for her having missed the meetings, but she didn't really believe he would: he was already sensitive to her moods, even considering the short time they had known each other.

"No problem," he said casually. "I took care of them, and I talked to Dorothy."

Cathy felt a twinge of guilt. "Steve, I had planned to. I didn't mean for you to do it."

"Honest, Cathy, I think she was actually relieved. In fact, she's been laboring over another offer she's had and this made the decision for her. She resigned as of today."

"So soon?"

"C'mon, let's go to the control booth," he said, taking her arm.

In the corridor on the way to the booth, Cathy felt him eyeing her, and then she heard him ask in an unsure tone, "Sorry about last night?"

Although the previous night had been on her mind constantly since waking, she really wasn't ready for his question. She thought furiously, her mind at war with her heart. Then, without looking at him, she heard herself say rather flippantly, "Sorry?" Of course not. You're a wonderfully exciting man."

He stopped in his tracks and roughly grabbed her arm. She turned to see his grimace.

"Wonderfully exciting?" His jaw tightened and his warm brown eyes turned to fire. "That must have been nice for you," he added sarcastically.

Now she was flustered. "Yes, Steve, it was."

As soon as she said it, she realized it wasn't what she meant or what he wanted to hear.

"Steve, can't we talk about this later...please? I've got a million things to do today."

She attempted to walk away, but he refused to let go of her arm.

"Just one quick question, Cathy. Have you known *many* wonderfully exciting men?" His head was tilted sideways; his eyes bore through hers as he waited for her slow-coming answer.

"I'm not a child, Steve," she said unfalteringly, "and having to give you a rundown of my love life is not in my contract."

"Neither was sleeping with me last night," he spit out quietly, but firmly.

She pulled her arm free and put on her glasses. Raising her chin slightly she said, "Don't make of it more than it was, Steve. You were in a bad way last night. I did what I could...to help. That's all."

"Being Florence Nightingale is not in your contract either," he said, his voice not so rough, his eyes examining hers as though he only half believed the cool façade she was putting up.

The green flecks in her hazel eyes glistened. "Florence had her rewards, Steve...and I had mine."

She stalked off and left him standing in the middle of the corridor, his mouth agape.

When Cathy entered the booth, it was in semidarkness, the bank of TV monitors alive and drawing the attention of the row of technicians flanking the director. She was about to plop herself down in humiliation—ashamed of what she had just implied to Steve.

"Cathy!"

The husky female voice from the other side of the room was familiar, but Cathy's mind was still seeing the look on Steve's face. She glanced across the room.

"Holly!"

They met halfway, embracing, eyes wide.

"Holly, I didn't expect you until this afternoon. God, it's good to see you again." Then, quietly she said, "I can use a friend around here. How's your sister?"

Holly beamed. Her long black hair, heavily streaked with gray, flared out like an Egyptian headpiece. "Just great, and she's thrilled to have a roommate again. She hates living alone. Would you believe she's got three locks on her apartment door. Three, mind you!"

The word *roommate* made Cathy wince, but Holly didn't notice. In fact, neither of the women noticed the man who had moved near enough to overhear Holly's remark.

"Roommates can add zest to an otherwise humdrum existence, can't they, Cathy?" he said smoothly.

She turned to find Steve leaning down, resting his hands on the back of her chair.

Holly was sharp; she didn't fail to notice the look in Steve's eyes, nor did she miss the poignant silence that set in.

Cathy mumbled something about assuming Steve and Holly had already met earlier that morning, and then she was thankful for the raspy "Sh!" that came from the technical director.

The audio man in the booth called down into the studio for a mike check on Vanessa. The three open cameras had various shots of her, which showed up on the monitors in the director's booth. Lying back in the bed on the set, she was going over her lines for the upcoming scene, the same scene that Ted Palmer had disrupted on Friday.

"Mike check, Vanessa." The hollow voice of the floor director was picked up on the boom mike over the bed and filled the control booth.

Vanessa looked at her script and read flatly, "Ralph, how can you hold me in your arms and tell me you still love your wife?" She smiled, looked up at the camera checking out a shot. "Okay?"

"Okay, sweet thing!" the audio man sent back, as Vanessa's mike continued to send studio noises into the control booth.

Just then, Ted Palmer, naked from the waist up, walked on set. His face formed his usual not-sure-where-I-am smile. "Hi, guys!" he belted out. "Anyone see Catherine the Great yet today? Maybe we're lucky and she's just here part-time."

His raucous laugh was cut short as Vanessa pointed gingerly to the boom mike above the bed.

The shots of the set and Ted's comments were all too apparent to the people in the control booth. As the technicians tried to catch a glimpse of Cathy's reaction—an icy glare at the monitor framing Ted's face—the director covered his eyes with the palm of his hand.

Cathy leaned toward Holly, whose jaw was dangling. "I need to talk to you about that person," she said menacingly.

At a little after one o'clock, Cathy, Holly, and Steve started down Fifth Avenue, heading for the restaurant where Steve had made reservations.

"I can't believe I'm back in New York," Holly blurted out, gaping at the skyscrapers while walking elbow to elbow with the throng moving like a determined herd. "Where else can you find such a fair field full of folk?...to quote somebody or other."

Steve took her arm and asked furtively, "Holly, have you been playing in the medicine cabinet?"

"What, and ruin a free lunch?"

She and Cathy were about to continue on down Fifth when Steve took hold of them and turned west on Forty-eighth, leading them into a restaurant, through a martini-clutching lunch crowd to a fairly quiet table in the corner.

"Three dry Rob Roys on the rocks," Steve said when their waiter arrived, and then added, "We'll order later."

"Hey, hey, you're my kinda guy." Holly's bright, gravelly voice matched the smile on her face.

Cathy wasn't smiling. "There you go again, Steve. First you decide where we're going to eat, and now you decide we want a Rob Roy."

"Don't you?"

The waiter turned back toward them and lifted a pencil, waiting.

"That has nothing to do with it," Cathy said. "It would have been more polite to ask before ordering for us."

"No problem here," Holly interjected.

"C.A., would you care for a Rob Roy?" Steve asked superciliously.

"On the rocks, please."

An annoyed waiter departed.

Holly eyed them both. "Are you sure *you two* haven't been playing in the medicine cabinet?"

"Attention, ladies," Steve ordered. "Let's decide on lunch. I would strongly recommend corned beef and cabbage."

"Sounds good to me," Holly agreed.

"Holly, you are one gal who's going to be very easy to get along with," Steve complimented. Then, looking at Cathy, "Corned beef?"

"No." She studied the menu. "I'll have the brandied skillet steak," she said sweetly, having chosen the most expensive item on the luncheon menu.

Steve's eyes rolled upward in their sockets in mock horror at the price. Then, to Holly, he joked, "Do you think you and I could split *one* corned beef?"

"Oh, brother." She slapped his thigh. "You just shot the hell out of your theory that I'd be easy to get along with. My body is up for negotiation, but my food, uh-uh."

With drinks set before them, Steve announced, "Okay, ladies, put on your thinking caps. This is a working luncheon. I'll referee." Then, surreptitiously to Holly, he said "I think you and I will be doing a lot of listening."

"Steve," Cathy said firmly, "if the vice-president of daytime programming wasn't after new input, I would be holidaying in Hawaii right now."

"And miss your brandied skillet steak?"

Ignoring his remark, she gave her attention to Holly.

"Holly, our writers are running a plot-line factory. We're saddled with papier-mâché heroes and women who jump into bed because they don't seem to have anything else to do."

Already wound up in her spiel, Cathy didn't notice the look on Steve's face when she spoke of women jumping into bed. She continued, "Our characters need a stronger sense of community. They have to have reason to know each other better and interact on a regular basis, even if their story-line crossover is minimal." She took a sip of her drink. "And the scenes, Holly, they're too long. The stories have to move much faster to keep an audience tuned in."

Holly put her glass down, her face all seriousness. "Right. I noticed that this morning. Today a three-page scene is considered long. Nobody thinks in terms of six- or seven-page scripts anymore."

"But," Steve broke in, "you can't get too complicated, either. The viewers have to keep track of more than one story line and have to understand the intricate cross-relationships between our people."

"Thought you were giong to referee, Steve," Cathy said dryly.

"Sorry." He picked up his drink.

Cathy batted her eyelids at him, turned to Holly, and went on. "We need a stronger balance of romance, action and humor—some playful one-liners, but the humor has to stem naturally from the characters' own lives...as it does in real life. What we're getting now would have been rejected in the days of vaudeville."

Holly looked over at Steve. "How come your friend here isn't writing? He seems like a quick thinker."

Lifting his glass to her, he said, "You're very perceptive, Holly."

"Now listen, you two," Cathy said seriously, "I don't want you getting buddy-buddy and raining on my production parade."

"C.A., we were just—" Then, realizing he was supposed to be only refereeing, Steve mumbled an apology.

"And we need some more glitz for our stories...some high-gloss backdrops, Holly."

"Budget, ladies, budget." He was serious. "I got sucked into a desperately needed downpour for a recent show that lasted less than a minute on the air to the tune of eleven thousand smackeroos."

Cathy glared at him. "We are not neophytes, Steve."

"I'm not at all concerned with your sexual preference. Just don't plan on going off the deep end of the balance sheet. Red ink brings out the beast in me."

"Apparently Rob Roys do, too," she added flippantly, leaning back in her chair, as if to show him she felt shut out.

Not missing her movement, Steve said, "And I've got a new, hotter-than-hot talent for you to develop, Holly: Devlin Howard."

Cathy shot back up in her chair, all ears, as Steve went on. "He's got looks, brains"—then, for Cathy's benefit—"and the loveliest blue eyes you could ever imagine."

"Can he act?" Holly asked with her usual frankness.

Steve angled a look at Cathy. "A person whose judgment I respect very much saw him on camera and said, "Who cares?""

Cathy squirmed quietly.

"Will he do seminude scenes?" Holly inquired.

"He will," Cathy interrupted, "and he'll do them beautifully." Her voice became more adamant. "And he does have talent. Holly, we do need more sex on 'SFL,' but in up-to-date situations, sex with reason, seminude scenes that suit a purpose, not just the voyeuristic field days that're being taped now. There's a newer audience out there, a more diverse audience that encompasses college students, business and professional people, and men, too. There's a bunch of closet soap opera addicts that no one even knows about...and we've got to get them watching 'SFL.'"

Steve and Holly both applauded her and then lifted their glasses in unison.

"One more word on the subject and I'm through—for now, anyway. Whatever we do put on the air has got to be wrapped up in a really heartwarming story that the audience can believe in, that they can identify with. Really, Holly, how many people do you personally know that have been shot?"

"None."

"That's exactly what I mean. But we all do know people who have been in love, and we've seen them do some pretty strange things, haven't we?"

"Right on, C.A." Steve broke in pointedly.

Holly watched Cathy's face muscles tighten. She glanced at Steve and then back to Cathy. At the moment, neither one seemed to be aware that she was even present. She began to tap her glass with her spoon as she sang, "I like New York in June—"

Luckily, before she had to continue, the waiter arrived, took their order and left them to redesign their favorite soap opera, "Search for Love."

Late that afternoon, Cathy had Holly sit in on the meeting she had with the four directors of "SFL." Holly was used to seeing Cathy in action, but she had never seen her go to it with such dynamism, and once they were alone in Cathy's office she let her know it.

"Cathy, I think you have two very unhappy directors on your hands."

"I also have two very happy ones, the better of the four."

"Don and Jason...you're right, they are jewels from the little I've seen them do so far, but you were brutal to the other two."

"And with good reason. When you see them at work you'll understand."

"That bad, huh?"

Cathy leaned forward at her desk. "Holly, you know me. I am not about to squelch anyone's creativity, but Dirk and Bob need to do better preplanning for their shots and they've got to stick with what they decide when they work over their scripts. This business of elaborate and time-consuming experimentation on the set costs us money. Sure, there's going to be some changes in any director's planned shots once he actually sees them on camera, but both of those guys are waiting until they've got live bodies in front of the lens before they do their heavy thinking."

She leaned back, toying with the gold chain around her neck. "Neither one of them sees anything wrong with having interrupted love scenes that are continued an hour later or even the next day, all because they haven't spent enough time visualizing the scene and making artistic decisions before walking into the studio." Leaning forward again, she pounded the desk. "They run the cast through a line rehearsal, a blocking, a run-through, and a dress rehearsal, and they *still* haven't decided what they're going to do with the damn cameras, never mind what lens they're going to use. It's not fair...not fair to the actors who often spend the previous night memorizing their parts...and it's not fair to Steve."

Holly's eyebrows raised. "Oh! I see."

"You see what?" she asked quizzically, leaning back in her chair.

"Oh, nothing. Uh. . .speaking of Steve. What's with you two? I had the feeling World War Three was about to break out at lunch."

Cathy picked up a pencil and began to roll it between her fingers. "You'll have to excuse him, Holly. He's had a bad year."

"Honey, I think Steve is charming. I was referring to you. Every time he opened his mouth you pounced on him. I mean your whole aura was blood red, just as it was at the meeting with the directors."

Cathy straightened in her seat, annoyed by Holly's frankness, but not really expecting anything else from the person she considered her closest friend. She started to defend herself, but changed her mind, realizing that she couldn't pretend with Holly. She slapped the pencil down on the desk.

"I had a bad night—I didn't get much sleep. Maybe my nerves are a little edgy."

"Edgy? I can count the little devils all over your skin." Holly studied Cathy's weak smile. "Want to tell Holly all about it?"

Cathy's deep sigh let her friend know that she was on the right track.

"Is something going on between you and Steve?" Holly asked cautiously.

"No!" came Cathy's quick reply.

"I don't understand why not. He's an extremely attractive man, inside and out, and you *are* living with him."

"That's just for business reasons. Haven't you ever seen 'Three's Company'?"

"Yeah, yeah. . .and I'm Maria Theresa of Austria."

"Holly, don't look for something that isn't there. Steve and I have a job to do here, and that's all that's going on."

"Does he know that?"

"Of course he does."

"You could have fooled me. I see the way he looks at you...like a starved man eyeing a feast."

Cathy got up, walked to the window, and turned to Holly. "I told you, he's had a bad year. A son who drowned, a divorce...that'd be enough to unsettle any man, make him look for comfort from any woman at hand."

"Any woman? Steve doesn't strike me as being that type, but then, I don't know him as well as you do, do I?"

"No, you don't, double-oh-seven, but knowing you—"

"Is to love me, right?"

"Holly, you and Steve would make a good pair. You're both candidates for the funny farm."

"One more interrogation and I'll back off." She lowered her eyes. "Does Steve know anything about you? About Jed and—"

"No, he doesn't!" Her voice rose in anguish. "And there's no reason he should."

The door to Cathy's office opened and Steve stuck his head in. "You two staying here all night?"

Holly got up. "I'm game if you can persuade Ted Palmer to keep me company." The deep sigh that followed told them she was only half kidding.

As she started to leave, Steve lowered his voice in confidentiality. "Holly, you'd best be prepared to fight lover boy off now that he knows you're the head writer."

"Fight him off? Are you insane? Dear God, where do you think I get my ideas for the love scenes I come up with?

Research, man, research.'' She went down the hall smiling to herself. ''Fight him off. . .ha!''

Cathy began to gather her things, knowing that Steve was waiting for her so they could leave together.

''I guess you can add Holly to your fan club, Steve. She's really taken with you.''

''And you. . .are you taken with me?'' he asked in a voice that told her he was serious.

''I admire you immensely, Steve. The more I see you in action around here, the more I feel I'm not really a necessity. You probably just needed someone to push a few of your buttons to get you started again.''

He held the door open while she walked past him. ''You may have pushed a few you hadn't intended to.''

She stopped and turned to see the enigmatic smile on his face. Then he took her arm.

''Let's go home, C.A.''

Chapter Eight

Behind her, Cathy heard the safety bolt being shoved into place with a little more zest than usual. Now that she was at home alone with Steve, without the diversions of the studio, she began to feel more uncomfortable.

Her one hope was that he wouldn't pursue the conversation he'd begun in the corridor at the studio, but knowing Steve, she knew she couldn't count on that. Perhaps, though, just perhaps, her intimation that the night they spent together was not of great importance to her, that she had just tried to be *of help*—perhaps he would let it go at that.

"I like Holly," he said with an animation that instantly relaxed her troubled thoughts. "Do all the girls in California have tans like you two?"

Cathy started up the stairway with her attaché case. Not sure why, she answered curtly, "Girls in California are pretty and healthy-looking...girls in New York are pretty and pale."

Following behind her, he let loose a low shrill whistle. "So, it's going to be one of those evenings."

Turning, she snapped, "Well, you asked didn't you?"

"I did? Oh, right. I did."

While changing her clothes, Cathy tried to understand just why she felt like all her nerve ends were jangling. Her mind seesawed with ideas: *I don't want to be here...I do; I hate him...I don't; I hate New York...no, I don't.*

Adjusting her French twist in the mirror she thought, "Well, at least you're too young to be going through menopausal madness."

A quick spray of cologne and she went downstairs, having heard Steve's cheerful whistling and the splatter of his shower water as she passed his bedroom door.

Sitting on the sofa, her fingernails began a rhythmic tapping on the marble-topped end table. *If I were in my own apartment, I wouldn't be sitting here waiting to find out just what I'm supposed to do next,* she thought impatiently, feeling put out that Holly was staying with her sister, knowing that they would have had a good time together as roommates.

"Doobie-doobie-doo," floated down the staircase at her. Looking up, she saw Steve bouncing down—wearing the skimpiest bathing suit she had ever seen.

In her work, Cathy had become blasé to the seminudity of hunks that had become an integral part of soaps—almost blasé, anyway. With all of Ted Palmer's high beefcake marks, she wouldn't touch him with a ten-foot pole, but the man coming toward her was another story.

At work she could assess male physiques much the same as she would inspect a prime roast at the butcher's. At work, the men never sent a chill streaking down her spine the way the sight of Steve was now doing.

Some men had a face that caused never-ending interest; some had chest and arm muscles that were appealing to the feminine eye; some had thighs that were strong and exciting, calves that were powerful and indicated an active nature—but, Steve, damn him, he had it all! *Why is he doing this to me?* she asked herself in confusion.

"Little late for sunning, isn't it?" she inquired sarcastically.

"But not too late for a dip in the hot tub," he answered politely, tugging at the oversized towel hanging around his broad shoulders, hiding the freckles she knew were there. "Join me?"

"Do I look Japanese?" she shot back at him.

"It'll relax you. . .not that you're not relaxed already, mind you." He tossed the towel down beside her on the sofa. "How about a drink?"

"No thanks," she said more reasonably, wishing he wouldn't stand in front of her like that, so very close.

Placing his strong hands on his hips, he unintentionally edged what little there was to his suit down even farther. "You know, C.A., you're an ideal roommate. . .never a bit of trouble." He took the vodka from the bar cart along with the ice bucket and went into the kitchen.

She listened as she heard him dump ice cubes in the bucket, as he popped the top off the tonic bottle, and then came his damn whistling as he went out on the deck, leaving the door slightly ajar.

Then she heard the Jacuzzi being uncovered and the *swoosh* of the hydro-massage jets. She waited and heard the sound of his body plopping into the water. At his satisfying "Ah!" she raced to the kitchen and began to fix herself a drink, only to be called midway.

"Cathy!"

She opened the door to the deck and looked down at him in the sunken tub, his arms stretched sideways, his face smiling smugly.

"I forgot my cigarettes. Would you?"

She went back inside and retrieved them from the table where he had put them.

"Here."

"Oh, and an ashtray...please."

Her face gave vent to her annoyance, but she came back with the receptacle and placed it noisily on the redwood next to him. "Anything else?"

"Why don't you come on in? Plenty of room."

Without answering, she stalked back inside and picked up a magazine.

"Cathy!"

"Ooooh!" she moaned, throwing the magazine down. "Now what?"

"Be a doll and switch on that nightlight."

Darkness had begun to set in, and as she switched the yellow light on, it covered him with a soft glow that instantly reminded her of the sheen his skin had taken on in the moonlight the previous evening. And those eyes of his, those warm, smiling—Damn, but he looked comfortable, leaning back, his legs floating full-length near the top of the gushing water.

He held up his empty glass. "Would you?" She took it from him. "And would you mind putting the stereo on? There's a speaker out here."

"Who was your last slave, Steve?" she asked caustically.

"If you were in here, I'd have to do all these things myself." His voice was oozing with suggestion.

"That's for sure."

"Get our drinks and come on in Cathy." His eyes turned serious. "We've got to talk."

She was hot, maybe from the August night air, maybe from all the running back and forth she had been doing for him. The tub did look inviting—and she knew they would eventually have to talk things out.

"When I get my chores done," she said dryly, taking his glass inside with her.

On her way upstairs to change, she punched the radio on and lowered the volume. In minutes she was back down in her two-piece swimsuit. She stopped in the kitchen to fix their drinks, and moments later she was cautiously hanging on to the side of the hot tub—across from Steve.

"This is nice," she admitted, feeling the jets of water pummel her skin.

"Stretch your legs out," he suggested.

The soft music from the speaker and the yellow light against the thick vines growing up the redwood latticework brought a soothing relaxation to her body, a relaxation she badly needed.

With half-opened eyes she watched him snuff out his cigarette in the ashtray—and then she saw it lying on the deck, the little piece of blue material that he called a bathing suit.

Swallowing a mouthful of water, she jerked herself to a standing position. "How dare you!" she spat out.

"What'd I do now?" he asked innocently.

"That!" She pointed to his discarded suit.

"I always do that." He pointed, too. "That's what a Jacuzzi is for: to relax."

"Can't you relax with something on?"

"No, not as well. Can you?"

"You bet I can." She started to lift herself out of the tub.

He reached for her arm. "Cathy, don't. If it makes you feel better, I'll put it back on, but I do want to talk to you." He reached for the suit and held it up. "But we're not in Saint Patrick's Cathedral, you know. . .we're in the Village."

Suddenly Cathy felt a little ridiculous. After last night, she told herself, she was hardly convincing sounding like a prude. "Never mind," she said quietly.

"Good." He tossed the suit aside. "Now we're getting somewhere."

"You're not getting anywhere, Steve. Don't delude yourself."

"That's not what I meant."

"What did you mean?"

"That we were beginning to sound like two adults, that's all." He handed her her drink and then reached for his own. Holding it up, he offered, "Let's start all over, okay?"

"Agreed," she said curtly, wishing she could take her eyes off the swimsuit that lay on the deck.

"Last night was a mistake, Cathy."

That surprised her, and immediately she knew that she wanted him to say something else—wanted him to try to talk her into renewing their intimacies, the closeness that she had felt with him; she wanted him to convince her that there was nothing wrong with two consenting adults having an affair, not in this day and age. She wanted him to be the aggressor, to take charge, to pursue her because his feelings for her were too strong for him to do otherwise; she wanted him to need her as—in her most honest thoughts— she knew she needed him.

A quick swallow of her drink and then she repeated, "A mistake?"

"For want of a better word," he said quietly. "I told you there would be no hanky-panky, and I'm sorry about last night."

"Sorry?" She felt like a fool echoing him the way she was doing, but her thoughts were a jumble of fears.

"That's not what I really mean." He was having trouble, too.

Cathy forced a weak smile. "We do seem to be having a problem understanding one another, don't we?"

"Yes, and that's not good," he said sorrowfully.

"I think I'd better find an apartment tomorrow, Steve," she said halfheartedly.

"That's not necessary! You know it's not." The roughness in his voice surprised her.

"It's what I *want* to do. Staying here is just not going to work out."

"Give it another day, Cathy, and then decide." His words came quickly and nervously.

"No."

"Twenty-four hours, then?" he pleaded.

He does want me! rushed through her brain, as though she were grasping for a life-saving device. She turned away from him, not wanting to see the tears that came so easily of late.

Yet, still not certain of herself, she began, "Steve, I don't think—"

"I know you don't," he interrupted. "That's why you've got to let me do some thinking for you. Sometimes you've got a blind spot as big as a TV tube."

"I do *not.*

She had turned quickly and he saw the tears in her eyes.

"Then why are you crying?"

"Women cry sometimes when they're happy, you know."

"That doesn't make sense."

"Well it does to us."

Wading over to her through the foaming water, he took her in his arms.

"Cathy, don't," he said soothingly. "I don't want you to ever be unhappy. Life's too short, and this isn't a dress rehearsal. This is it...all we're going to get." He pressed her head against his shoulder and ran the palm of his hand up and down her back. "We've got something special between us, C.A., something too precious not to take care of, and I'm willing to do it on your terms."

For a moment Cathy stood there rigidly, her palms pressed behind her against the rounded wall of the tub. She was silent and he was silent; only the soft sound of music and the gurgling of the water filled the dark night air. However her mixed emotions confused her, she was sure of one thing—that being this close to him gave her the greatest feeling of happiness she had ever experienced in her life.

Wanting to be closer, her slender arms slipped around his body and her fingers pressed into the smooth wet skin of his back. At the same moment that her hands touched him, she felt his excited body lean against hers and force her against the side of the tub, felt his fingers deftly undo the ties at her neck and back, felt him slip her top from her, letting it be carried away across the whirling water.

"God, you're beautiful," he whispered.

No one had ever told her she was beautiful before—no one else had ever looked at her in just that way. She had gotten so used to hiding behind her horn-rims and bun, gotten so used to bettering the men she worked with, so used to avoiding even the chance of an emotional commitment, that she had never allowed herself to be beautiful, not the way she felt now. And now, as he looked at her, smiling that vulnerable smile of his, she felt beautiful and wanted to be beautiful for him, for herself; and she wanted him to want her.

"I want you so much, Cathy," he said, kissing her ear and then her hair.

Good Lord! she wondered, *can he read my mind, too?*

He held her tightly, rubbing his wet chest against her smooth breasts. "I want you in the middle of breakfast, at night in bed, and I think I'll get an inside lock for my office door. We can have lunch together, and I'll want you then, too."

His constant rubbings and the undulations of his thighs against her were driving her crazy, sending wild messages to every hormone in her body. Resting her head against his shoulder, she lowered her hands to his backside and began her own intimate rubbings.

"You're supposed to be a dignified man of forty, Steve," she said playfully.

She felt him push the bathing suit from her hips and lean to her once again.

"Do I feel like a dignified man of forty?"

"You feel wonderful," she murmured, letting her fingers trace loving pathways around his firm buttocks and hard thighs, moving them around his waist and downward to his hardened masculinity.

"You make me crazy, Cathy. . .every time you touch me."

The next instant his lips were on hers, his breath mingling with hers; his movements against her became more forceful.

Then, with his lips brushing across hers, she heard him say, "I love you, Cathy. Please. . .love me back."

As Steve's tongue began its sensual dance with hers, Cathy felt his heartbeat grow stronger—or was it hers? Guiding him deep into the core of her soul, she locked her legs around his body, the palms of her hands alive with the thrill of the feel of him.

The swirling of the water became a rushing rapids as his gasps of delight mingled with the music that now sounded to her like a full symphony. A thrust—another—and yet another, the strongest, and then a unisoned spasm that slowly ebbed away, mixing with the magic of the warm summer night.

Moments later, he lay back in the tub and pulled her on top of him, resting his head on its edge, gripping the side with one strong arm, his other still about her, holding her securely.

"You and your aquatic pursuits," she said softly. "There's probably not a soul near here watching TV."

"So? It's prime time now. What do we care?"

His free hand continued to hold her, to move slowly up and down her back, his fingers pushing and squeezing her gently.

"What about dinner?" she asked.

He stood up in the water, letting her down smoothly. "Always thinking of eating." His hands started as far down her legs as they could reach and began a slow path toward her breasts. "Still, it looks good on you."

Laying her palms against his chest, she began to finger the wet brown hair, moving her tips to his nipples and then reaching upward around his neck. "We've got to keep your strength up, don't we, S.B.?"

"You little vixen." He thought a moment. "Hey, that'd be a great line for Vanessa."

Cathy pushed herself away from him. "That's not what I had in mind." Looking for the bottom of her suit, she found it and stepped into it. "Let's eat. . .I'm starving. Hand me my top, will you?"

"Why? Who's to see? He was serious.

"Steve Bronsky, if you think I'm going to stand up there half-naked and dry off, you've got another think coming. My top!"

Her two-piece in place, Cathy lifted herself out and dried herself with Steve's towel, noticing that he was watching her every move. And then a devilish twinkle set in her eyes.

She walked back and picked up his suit, took the towel, and laid it across the lounge chair on the other side of the deck. Twirling his suit in the air on her finger, she threw him a backward glance. "Coming?"

"Cathy! My suit! The towel at least. . .something!" he stammered.

Before closing the French doors, she stuck her head out. "This is the Village, Steve, not Saint Patrick's Cathedral."

Cathy's microwaved lasagna, green salad, and red wine had tasted delicious and now she lay sideways on the sofa, her head propped on her angled arm, the fingers of her one hand twisting Steve's brown waves into little curls as he sat on the carpet, his back against the sofa, his eyes closed.

"How long were you married, Steve?"

"Fourteen years...why?"

She had been right. "I was just curious." Then, running her fingers under the loose collar of his robe, she said "What happened between you and Meredith?"

He reached up and placed his hand over hers, pressing it against his neck. "I met her when I was in the service in Italy. I was young. Maybe it was the uniform that attracted her."

Not on your life, Cathy thought to herself.

"And Meredith, well, she was like no other woman I had ever met. She oozed charm and culture. She and Louise, her mother, were making their obligatory tour of the world, and there in Italy, in the middle of a performance of *Madama Butterfly* at La Scala in Millan, I got the socks knocked off me. We thought we were soulmates, but New Yorkers...she from the East Side, and me from across the park." He looked up at Cathy, then he glanced back across the room "Louise didn't like that one bit, but a year later we were married. After my stint in Vietnam we settled in that Sutton Place apartment you saw."

"With Louise?"

"*With* Louise," he affirmed. "About ten years ago I bought this house." He chuckled quietly. "You know, I thought we were one helluva family...two great kids."

"What changed it all?"

Steve turned sideways and rested his head against the sofa, letting his hand slip up over Cathy's thigh. "It was probably as much my fault, but I was working night and day to make my own way instead of taking it easy and letting us live off of Meredith's money. She got bored when we stopped having, and going to, dinner parties. Then she and Louise would run off to Europe. They just had to be in Paris in the spring. It was quite a while before I knew that Franklin Rimbaud also liked Paris in the spring. Funny thing about it is that in our business extramarital affairs are so easy, and, I've always thought, so unsatisfying, and there was Meredith in Paris with Rimbaud."

"Steve, if you don't want to—"

"No, Cathy, I want to get it out. I've never really talked to anyone about all this before." He sat up and faced her. "About a month after Stevie drowned, Louise died. I guess Meredith had had too much grief at one time, but one night she just came out and told me that she wanted a divorce...that she couldn't stand me anymore, that life was just one big joke to me, that my work in television was meaningless. Fourteen years, and I never knew how she really felt about me. Fourteen years and then we said good-bye."

Cathy leaned down and kissed his head. "Life is full of sad good-byes, isn't, Steve?" she said a little too quietly.

He turned quickly, hearing the vague tone of suffering in her voice, and when he saw that her thoughts had wandered off, he had the feeling that she was hiding some secret from him. Taking her hand in his, he promised, "No good-byes for us, Cathy. . .right?"

Placing her hand on his cheek, she affirmed, "No, Steve, not for us." But, something inside her stirred and she had to ask herself if she really meant it—or was she merely comforting him again?

She looked down and saw that he had closed his eyes under the soothing strokes of her delicate fingers. "Tired?"

"Tired!" His eyes popped open. "I fell asleep jogging in place on the deck this morning."

She tapped his head. "Go to bed."

"You coming?" he asked quietly.

"No. I'm going to do the dishes, and then *I* am going to get some sleep."

"Hey!" Suddenly he took hold of her hand. "Will you look at that."

"What?" she asked nervously.

Studying her palm, he replied, "Your love line. It goes halfway up your arm!"

She pulled her hand from his. "Go to bed."

"Okay, Big Mamma." He slapped her playfully and got up. "Night."

Cathy watched him trot up the stairs and whispered to herself, "Good night, Steve."

With the dishes done, Cathy set up the coffee machine for the morning and checked the safety locks on the door to the deck. She should have been tired, too, she knew, but she wasn't. She turned down the volume on the stereo until it was barely audible. Sitting in the easy chair she began to reflect on the events of the past few days.

So quickly, she reminisced, so quickly had her life been set on a course she had been determined to steer it away from. Steve was wonderful, everything she could want in a man—and he had a thirteen-year-old son, the exact age that— She jumped up and pushed the off button on the stereo, turned out the lights, and noiselessly ascended the stairs. Pausing at Steve's door, she could hear his deep breathing. Good, she thought, he needs to sleep.

Alone in her bed, her arm across her forehead, she suddenly felt a sense of panic, a sense of being too vulnerable, but Steve would never hurt her, she told herself, not intentionally.

But she had been hurt, deeply hurt, almost half her life ago, and in all that time the wound had not healed. Not only hadn't it healed, it had festered, and the soreness was a force driving her—driving her with such compulsion that everything she did was a success, everything but loving another human being. She wasn't sure exactly when—she had a good idea—but at some point in her life she had said ''never again!''

From that point on she had guarded her emotions like the Iron Maiden she had been known as in college. From that time, her affairs had never been love affairs; they had been quick forays into the forbidden world of love, but so quick and guarded were they that she had always returned unscathed by Cupid's arrow.

But what should she do now? Should she let down her guard, let fall the drawbridge to the heart that was once almost shattered with a tearful good-bye in the past, a good-bye that had almost destroyed her?

Cathy eased herself onto her stomach and looked into the moonlight sifting through the sheer panels of her window.

"I couldn't take another good-bye from someone I loved, especially Steve," she murmured into her pillow, half-asleep.

What was it she had told Steve to comfort him? *Life is full of sad good-byes.*

No, she decided, the risk was too great. She was sure she would be unable to stand the pain of losing someone she loved again. And Steve was strong. He'd had a difficult time, but he was a survivor.

With eyes slowly closing, Cathy swore that she, too, would survive, but in her own way.

Chapter Nine

In the kitchen, as Cathy began readying the scrambled eggs, she listened patiently for one iota of good news from the morning news show, but the international, national, and local stories only depressed her, let alone the weather report that warned of temperatures approaching the hundred degree mark.

Annoyed, she punched the off button on the TV and turned on the FM radio station. Steve came bounding down the stairs, the curved tails of his dress shirt not quite covering his Jockey shorts. Seeing Cathy, he stopped abruptly.

Surprise and inquisitiveness shaded his features and his voice. "Oh...do I know you?"

"I see you're rested," she said. "Coffee's already plugged in, so go finish dressing. Breakfast is just about ready."

"Yes, ma'am." Back up he went without an argument.

Minutes later, his entry into the dining room preceded a quick kiss on Cathy's cheek, a kiss that was casual enough to him, but a gesture that left little pin pricks dotting her skin.

"You know," he remarked, biting off a piece of wheat toast, "getting up in the morning has been so much easier since you moved in. I'm getting used to your being around here."

During the silence that followed, Cathy knew he wanted her to say something that would tell him she felt the same way. He wasn't even looking at her—just dipping his fork into the scrambled eggs—but she knew he was waiting.

Sitting there across from her, freshly shaven, he looked so attractive, so energetic in a striped dress shirt opened at the neck, his wavy hair not yet fully in place; but it was the too-energetic chewing, the nervous dabbing with his napkin at the jelly at the corner of his mouth that assured her he was waiting for some response from her.

"There's something I've got to say, Steve," she began slowly.

"No. . .don't say it."

"Why not?"

"Whenever someone says 'There's something I've got to say,' I've found I don't want to hear it."

She poured them both more coffee. "We're rushing things, Steve. Too much is happening too fast. It's making me nervous."

He sat back in his chair as though trying to decide if the woman across from him was the same lady he had spent the previous evening with. Running his tongue across his upper teeth, his lips tightly closed, he looked at her intently.

"You know you're a bust as far as breakfast chitchat is concerned, don't you?"

"Five days, Steve!" she blurted out. "Five days and we're living together and twice we've—"

"Made love?" he asked dryly.

Eyes lowered, her head swept back and forth in confusion. "I can't take it that lightly. I've got to understand why I'm doing what I'm doing. I've got to be certain it's the right thing. I've got to be sure of myself. I've got to think ahead, to know where this is going to lead."

"One question, Cathy. Why?"

"Why what?"

"Why the big change since last night?"

"I haven't changed, Steve. It's just that I see things a little clearer in daylight."

He rested his arms on the table's edge and leaned toward her. "Maybe you should get a night job," he suggested caustically, "and sleep during the day."

"Be serious for once, Steve."

"I *am* being serious."

Cathy threw her napkin on the table and started to gather the dishes. "It's just that this...this relationship of ours has to cool down."

"We should live like brother and sister, you mean."

"Yes...for a while, anyway."

"Well, I guess I can get used to being a bruver."

"A bruver?"

"Yeah...a brother who really wants to be a lover...but you're going to be ridiculous as a sisver."

She ignored his attempt at humor, "It's that or nothing, Steve." She took the dishes and headed for the kitchen.

The cab ride to the studio was silent. Once there, Steve's parting words lashed out at her.

"You know, C.A., you're looking at your dragons through one big magnifying glass."

Holly had just opened the door from the writers' offices, just in time to hear his parting shot and see him stalk off, leaving a flustered Cathy standing in the corridor.

"You bothered by dragons this morning, Cathy?" she asked cautiously.

"Oh, don't pay any attention to him. He's chock full of one-liners."

Holly nodded toward the writers' offices behind the closed door. "I sure could use him in there. I haven't seen such upset since they changed class schedules on me in college."

"Holly, if any of the writers aren't going to be flexible and productive, get rid of them. This is not a retirement home for hacks."

"Oh, I like that. Mind if I write it down?"

"While you're at it, write this down, too." She started down the corridor toward her office and Holly followed. "The two bedrocks of soap opera are greed and lust. 'SFL' scripts have just been alluding to greed, and the dialogists' idea of lust is a hunk hitting on a thankful twit of a female."

Inside her small cubicle of an office, Cathy shut the door behind them, threw her handbag and case on her desk, and sank into her chair.

"Women have desires, pent-up needs, physiological urges, Holly. . .just like men!"

"How did you have your iron nails this morning, Cathy—over easy?"

Holly knew Cathy well, very well. She had known her ever since Cathy had first been shipped off to California by her father, and she knew why he had done so; she had seen Cathy through the bad days that had almost destroyed her. As Cathy sat across from her, ranting and raving, Holly knew it wasn't just the show she was concerned about.

Cathy leaned forward in her chair. "I'm not talking about breakfast, Holly, I'm talking about love and the way men use women."

"You don't have to tell me, Cathy. Armies have marched over me, and I've loved every minute of it."

Cathy smiled for the first time that morning. "Well, we can't go so far as to put your love life on the air...but we've got to give our women a more normal eighties characterization. I don't mean have a bunch of wild-eyed nymphomaniacs leering out of the TV screens in people's homes, but we've got to dig into the decisions women are having to make these days."

"Like living in sin?" Holly suggested knowingly.

Cathy blanched. "Well...for one thing, yes." She fingered the bun at the back of her head. "But highlight the problems of an arrangement like that. And," she added strongly, "I don't buy this business of the 'Three's Company' premise that all can be sweet and pure when men and women live under the same roof."

"Oh?" More insight on Holly's part.

"Our stories should show that it's not easy for a woman nowadays. I don't care how old or how young she is. It's still a man's world. They don't have to worry about their reputations, but, like it or not, we do."

To Holly, it seemed that Cathy was talking more to herself than for her benefit as head writer. She listened as her friend continued her tirade, her arms flailing the air.

"A man beds down and he's macho, a woman does the same thing and she's a tramp. The double standard is still all around us."

"She's the one who gets pregnant...he doesn't," Holly added, sorry the minute she said it.

"And is that fair?" Cathy asked, her reason beginning to slip.

"No, my dear, but it is a physiological fact we'd best keep in mind."

"Coffee?" Cathy asked, seeing that the water in her small electrical pot was boiling.

"No, trying to cut down."

"You should cut down on the smokes," Cathy advised, watching Holly reach for another cigarette.

"Let's skip my health and talk shop, boss lady."

"Another thing, Holly, we've been hitting it hard on teenage romance all summer because the kids are out of school, but now we need to focus on stories that are pertinent to all viewers...include twenty-year-old love, thirty, forty." Cathy's face softened. "Forty," she repeated as she went through a private reverie. "Uh...did I say forty?" she asked absently.

"You did. Twice."

"Well, love can be very beautiful at forty, Holly. At that age, people are experienced. They know what they want. They're extremely selective." She leaned back in her chair, looking relaxed for the first time. "They can be tender, exciting...utterly fascinating...."

Holly put her pencil down, crossed her legs and then her arms, half smiling as she watched Cathy's businesslike mask change to the face of a woman in love. Suddenly Cathy noticed that Holly was examining her.

"Uh...forty, yes, and fifty- and sixty-year-old love, too. Everyone needs love, Holly, and 'SFL' is going to give it to them every weekday."

"Back down to earth, Cathy. You know geriatric love is taboo on TV. Get an audience with mainly people over fifty and it's no-go with the sponsors. By the way, I need to know, any special taboos at this network?"

Cathy thought as she sipped her instant coffee. "No nuns...unless they fly. No astrology. Half the audience believes in it, and the other doesn't. No matter what you do, you lose half. No incest, not yet, anyway."

Her index finger went up in the air. "But we do need sex...up to the line of having a blue-pencil war with that prude from Broadcast Standards and Practices. Have you met her yet?"

"Unfortunatley," Holly answered, having hit head-on with Standards people before.

"Just keep her off my back, Holly, please."

"Oh my, rank doth have its privileges, doesn't it?"

"Exactly."

"And what about Vanessa? You said you wanted to give her character more dimension."

"Oh yes. I've got to talk to her today." Cathy jotted herself a note. "I think she's being wasted, Holly. Come up with something that gets to her...hurts her. Let the viewers see that she can suffer just like the good gals, but don't overdo. She has to revert to the behavior life has conditioned her to...react with. Well, you know what I mean."

"Did you ever get to casting about the people for the Martinez and Jefferson couples you want written in?"

"Why does that day have only twenty-four hours in it, Holly? I'll take care of that today; it's important. We've got to get some ethnic groups on 'SFL'...it's too damn lily-white. This country's no longer a melting pot, it's a salad bowl, and everyone in it falls in and out of love."

Holly snuffed out her cigarette. "How hard to you want us to push Devlin?"

"Have you met him?"

"Have I ever! Oh, to be ten years younger and have him obligated to me. Mercy!"

"What do you think?"

"Well, I'm with you. In real life he's got something that turns my head, but will it happen on camera? I checked his background. No acting whatsoever."

"Listen, Holly, any man that looks like that, who has a background in political science and law and leaves Yale to try his hand at acting, has got to have a drive strong enough to move L.A. a little closer to Frisco."

"How should we treat him—good guy or fink?"

Cathy sat back in her chair, turning her coffee mug in her hand. "He strikes me as a young Bogart, young Garfield type. Taller and handsomer, but, you know, hard on the outside, with intense sensitivity under the surface. At the beginning let's keep his scenes limited to two or three people at the most. I don't want that face of his getting lost in a mob shot. Lots of close-ups will get the audience's attention."

Holly's eyes lit up. "How about pairing him with Vanessa? Let him be the one who reached her heart for a change...then have him drop her for someone else. She could suffer and then do bad things to get back at him.''

"Good. That sounds real good. He worked well with Vanessa on camera the other day.'' Thinking, she narrowed her eyes. "And that would take care of two birds with one stone. Holly, you're brilliant.'' She thought some more. "Oh, God, I'm going to say this, but Vanessa will...well, you know what she'll do when she reads the script, but here goes. Holly, highlight the age difference. You know, the older woman and the younger man bit. Vanessa looks terrific, but she's been around so long her fans must know she hasn't seen her twenties for some time. She'll be great, though, and it'll give her a chance to broaden her range in the part.''

Holly scribbled her notes while asking, "Do you think that Devlin would work two shifts for a while?''

Before Cathy could answer, her office door opened slightly after two polite knocks.

"Miss Arensen? Oh...I didn't know you were busy.''

"No problem. Come on in, Devlin. You know Holly.''

He nodded. "I met Miss Lange this morning.''

"Cathy and Holly, Devlin. We're all family here,'' Cathy said sincerely. "What can I do for you?''

"I just signed my new contact with Mr. Bronsky.'' He angled a look at Holly and then his smiling eyes went back to Cathy. "I just wanted to thank you.''

Holly got the message. "I was just about to leave, Devlin. Hold your thanks just a sec.'' Then she said to Cathy, "What are you doing for lunch?''

Cathy glanced over her desk. "Working, I'm afraid.''

"Catch you later, then.''

"Go get those scribes," Cathy joked as Holly closed the door behind her.

"Sit down, Devlin." She folded her hands and leaned forward. "How does it feel to know you're going to be daytime TV's latest heartthrob?"

"Great, just great, Miss...uh...Cathy."

"Don't let me down, Devlin, I've been singing your praises and I want you to come though for me."

Devlin's blue eyes glowed, misinterpreting Cathy's remark. "Gratitude is my middle name."

She looked up at him uneasily. "I don't want your gratitude, Devlin. I want your sweat." She tapped her pencil lightly on the desk. "Did you feel comfortable with Vanessa...in bed, I mean?"

"Very."

"Good. We're going to pair you with her for a start. I'll get Holly to outline your character for you. We'll give you some extra time at the beginning, but after that you're on your own, just like everyone else."

"I won't disappoint you. I'll be whatever you want me to be."

"Keep the perm, Devlin. On you it looks good." She eyed his tank top, which seemed molded to his muscular chest; noted the smoothness of his well-formed shoulders and arms. "You look good in casuals, but I want you to go to wardrobe. Get fitted for some suits." Another note jotted down.

As she wrote, she didn't see the slight arching of Devlin's eye, nor the upward curve of one corner of his mouth.

"One piece of advice."

"Yes?" he said quickly.

"We've got four regular directors on 'SFL,' some better than others. At times, it's going to seem to you that they're trying to pull your character in four different directions, and unforunately that will happen...but listen to them. Don't make verbal suggestions to them about the way *you* think a scene should be shot. Let them block it out for you. You spend your energy looking good in the close-ups. And don't play the scenes for yourself, play them for, and to, whomever you're working with."

He hunched forward in his chair and rested his bare arms across his jeans. "Yes, ma'am," he said, smiling at her a little too intimately.

Yes, ma'am, she remembered, was one of Steve's ways of addressing her.

"If you have any problems, I want to hear about them first. Understood?"

"Understood."

"Okay, that's about it for now. Good luck."

He got up and went to the door. With his hand on the knob, he turned. "Cathy—"

She glanced up, wondering what it was he wanted. "Yes?"

"I was going to ask you to have lunch with me...a thank-you lunch, but I heard you tell Holly you'd be working."

"I will be, but thanks. Another time, okay?"

"Okay."

Between his *okay* and the time he was able to open the door to her office, Cathy's mind worked furiously. Steve had told her he had gotten used to her being around the house—too used to it, she thought.

"Devlin wait a minute."

He stepped back in and closed the door.

"How about a thank-you drink after work?"

If she thought his eyes were bright before, they now lit up like blue diamonds. Leaning against the door he saw her ruffle some papers on her desk.

"Let's see, the master sheet shows you free at four o'clock." A frown settled on her face. "I won't get out of here until well after six and I need to pick up a few things at a department store."

Hooking his thumbs in his jeans, he suggested, "I could meet you at six, six-thirty."

"Fine. Let's say six-thirty, downstairs in the lobby."

Cathy's breathing had quickened, not because of her date with Devlin, but because she knew she had put fire under her idea that Steve had to realize she did not belong to him, that he did not belong to her. But she quickly dismissed Steve from her thoughts and began to wade through the problems of supervising a daily hour-long soap.

Later that afternoon, when Cathy told Steve she had some shopping to do, he offered to be her guide. When she declined, she saw his mouth twitch anxiously. No subways, he warned her, not alone. And when she told him to go ahead with dinner without her, she had to convince him she was not running away from home.

Purposefully, Cathy let the one drink with Devlin extend to dinner, during which time she kept the conversation on business, destroying any hopes he had of expressing his gratitude to her in more personal ways.

And when she did begin her cab ride home, she was sure that Steve would have gone to bed; her watch told her it was almost twelve-thirty. To her, there seemed to be something magical about after midnight, something almost unrespectable about arriving home after twelve when the next day had already started, something that would obviously tell Steve that her life was not irretrievably wrapped up in his.

The taxi pulled away and for a moment she stood motionless, her face bathed in the yellowish light coming from the lamppost at the foot of the stairs. Then, finding the key Steve had given her, she unlocked the heavy door, stepped inside and quietly slipped the safety bolt in place.

She saw that he had left the light on in the foyer for her. Turning it off, she crossed the squared linoleum with silent steps. At the living room arch, she saw him.

Chapter Ten

He was just sitting there in the semidarkness and silence of the room, the bottle of Calvados close at hand. Only the lamp on the other side of the room was lit. Still wearing the striped dress shirt he had on at breakfast, buttons half undone, sleeves rolled up quarter length, he blew a strong stream of blue smoke from between his pursed lips and then leaned back on the sofa and crossed his legs.

"Good morning," he said cheerfully.

Cathy swallowed hard. Then, bracing herself, she entered the living room and put her one package and handbag on an easy chair.

"I didn't think you'd still be up."

"What kind of a brother would I be if I didn't worry about you?. . .sister."

Whatever it was that she heard in his voice, it frightened her, and it wasn't fair, she told herself. She had made it clear at breakfast that there was no commitment between them. Why was he sitting there in the dark waiting for her?

She glanced at the Calvados, and seeing its contents had diminished significantly she looked at him. His face was flushed and intense.

"You certainly have a healthy glow, Steve."

"Comes from drinking lots of milk and having straight, white teeth."

"The Calvados helps, I imagine," she said curtly as she went into the kitchen to ready the coffee machine for the morning. He had already done it.

"Well, it's late, Steve. Good night."

She started to pick up her package and handbag. He leaned forward.

"Aren't you going to tell me where you've been?" He crushed his cigarette in the ashtray with too much force.

Holding up her one package, she said, "Shopping."

"Well now, that was quite a spree. Tell me, do you find New York salesclerks to be a bit slower than those in California?" he asked, his eyes flashing sarcastically.

"Aren't you being a little theatrical, Steve?"

"We are in show business, aren't we?"

She threw the package back down on the chair. "All right, *brother*. I also had a drink with Devlin."

"Ummm. . .the plot thickens. Nice *young* man, that Devlin. How old is he? Twenty-three. . .twenty-four?"

His sarcasm was beginning to annoy her. "And we had dinner together."

Watching him refill his glass, she was sorry she had blurted that out the way she did, because she had learned that Steve's witticisms were sometimes used as a protective device when he was hurting.

He held up the Calvados bottle.

"No thanks."

"Coke?"

Something cool sounded good to her. "I'll get it," she said, starting to get up from the chair she had just sat down in.

"Goodness no! You've had a big evening. You must be exhausted...from all that shopping." He started for the kitchen.

"Thank you," she said overpolitely.

Turning to her, he fawned, "I'm a gentleman from the *old* school."

After returning with her Coke, he sat back down on the sofa.

The quiet got to her. "What have you been doing all evening?"

"Cheating at solitaire...what else?" He paused, his eyes blinking. "Think I was pining away for you?"

Cathy banged her Coke down on the table. "Steve, I don't want you pining away for me!"

"Well...not exactly pining." He lit another cigarette. "What did you have for dinner?"

"Chinese food," she answered dryly.

He thought a moment. "I didn't know you liked Chinese."

"I don't."

"Then why'd you have dinner with him?"

"I didn't know I was going to. I hadn't planned on it."

"Anything else happen...you didn't plan on?"

"Nothing."

She thought she saw his face muscles relax a little. Then he went into the study and brought back a little strip of paper and handed it to her.

"Here, put this in your shoe."

She took it gingerly. "What is it?"

"Our phone number," he said snidely, and sat down again.

"I *know* our phone number!" She crumpled the paper up and threw it toward him, but it didn't go very far.

Another quiet spell.

"Our friend, Devlin Howard," Steve then asked, "Is he a gentleman?"

"If you mean did he make love to me, the answer is no."

He crossed his knee with his ankle. "That sounds too much like the truth to be true," he said to himself, but loud enough to be heard.

Cathy rose to her full height, all five-feet-four. With hands on her hips, she demanded, "What's with you, Bronsky? You're not my father!"

Up he jumped, hands on his hips. "Well I'm damn well not your brother, either!"

"Oh!" she groaned, grabbing her things and making for the stairway. Halfway up she turned to him. "Tell me, Steve, at what age is it that little boys are supposed to grow up?"

"Tell *me*, Cathy," he said, his voice low and painful, "at what age do women learn to take a man's heart from the depths of despair, raise it up to the heavens and then dash it down into darkness again?"

Standing alone in the middle of the darkened living room, his arms hanging listlessly, he looked so miserable that Cathy wanted to run to him, wanted to hold his face in her hands, to kiss him, to bring back the smile that suited him so well—but she didn't. If she was afraid that loving him would make her suffer, well, she was suffering now, and that seemed to prove a point to her: loving meant suffering and losing, and saying good-bye. The only illogic in her thinking was that she wasn't losing Steve; she was driving him away.

"I..." Her words came with difficulty. "I'm not dropping you, Steve. I just need some time. If I've hurt you, I didn't mean to."

He moved to the staircase and rested his arms on the banister. "My God, Cathy, don't worry about it. I've just got this funny thing about rejection."

"I'm not rejecting you! I just need some space." She leaned her weary body against the wall on the staircase. "I knew this would happen. Moving in here was a big mistake, Steve. It hasn't worked out."

"I thought we were doing pretty well until tonight."

"That's just it. We were doing too well, acting like two youngsters playing at love." She dug her teeth into the inside of her lower lip and then forced the words out. "I'm not in love, Steve, and neither are you."

He ran his fingers through his disheveled hair. "Wow! And I thought finding out there was no tooth fairy was heavy."

"Will you be serious!" she shrieked.

"What is it you want me to do, Cathy. Take to the bottle? Smoke myself to death? I've had a year of that and it doesn't work. And then you showed up and each day became a memory day for me, each morning was like waking to a new adventure because you'd be there. If that isn't love, then—"

"Steve," she began softly, "you were hurting and I was a distraction. You lost a wife—"

"I don't miss Meredith," he interrupted.

"And you lost a son. I know how you feel about—"

The tension within him reached its breaking point. His face reddened and he flared, "How would you know what it's like to lose a son?"

The color drained from Cathy's face. She staggered and grabbed for the banister, wincing at the pain of the verbal knife that he had thrust deep into her heart.

He saw her blanch, saw her unsteadiness. "Cathy? Are you all right?"

The damage was done. She felt the dizziness come over her. Calling upon all the strength she had and cajoling more from some unknown reserve, Cathy smiled weakly and picked up the package she had dropped at her feet.

"You're right, Steve." Her voice was weak, colorless. "How could I possibly understand the pain of losing a child."

She turned away from him, her eyes glossy. Holding on to the banister for support, she slowly made her way upstairs.

"Cathy," Steve called softly, but she never heard him.

Sometime during the night, her eyes still red from the tears she had shed, Cathy heard a gentle knock on her locked bedroom door.

"Cathy." His voice was soft. "I've got to talk to you."

She turned her head away, stared toward the weak light sifting through her window.

"Cathy. . .please!"

She listened as he tried the knob and then banged on the door. Her hands flew up to cover her ears, and again the tears came. Moments later, all was quiet, but peaceful sleep evaded her, and for Cathy the night was long.

Lying there in semiconsciousness, she clutched at the pillow under head. Drifting into an uneasy limbo, her mind reviewed that day long ago in California when she convinced her Aunt Elizabeth to attend her son's wedding in Seattle, telling her that the baby wasn't due for almost two weeks.

"Famous last words," she mumbled in her half-sleep as she continued to recall snatches of the past, remembering the surprise of the gush of water that broke loose not long after her aunt had left for the airport, the frantic phone call to her doctor, the rush to the hospital in a taxi, and the long and difficult labor.

Weak and exhausted from the ordeal, Cathy's eyes had beamed as they placed the healthy baby boy on her bosom. Feeling his little fingers clutch around one of hers, she'd absorbed the beauty of the helpless miracle.

"You're going to have a mother and a father, and you're going to be loved very much," she'd whispered to her little son.

As Cathy's troubled sleep deepened, she relived the visit by the social worker from the adoption agency.

"As the biological mother, Catherine, you must make sure you have considered all aspects of surrendering your baby and that you truly want to do so."

Her eyes dulled, Cathy merely nodded to the young lady standing at her bedside.

"In that case, we've processed all the legal papers of surrender and adoption, and you're fortunate. The adoptive parents are willing for you to contact them periodically if you want to."

Silent, almost not hearing, Cathy shook her head.

"Catherine," the young woman asked, "are you feeling all right?" Peering dubiously into Cathy's sallow face, she repeated, "Catherine?"

Was it a minute later, was it a day? Cathy couldn't remember, but two doctors were at her bedside, talking to her. She wanted to answer, but she couldn't speak.

"Catherine, some women do experience a slight post-partum depression, but it doesn't last."

She felt his fingers spread her eyelids: he seemed to be staring at her.

Then the other doctor spoke. "Catherine, you seem to be having trouble speaking. Don't you want to talk to us?"

Cathy felt as if she were in a cocoon, separated from the two men and the nurse in white, and her new world was quiet, peaceful. All she wanted was for them to leave her alone. She didn't want to think about anything or anyone ever again, but their voices continued and she heard the nurse speak to one of the doctors.

"She hasn't eaten in two days and doesn't respond to any of the nurses or her aunt."

One doctor flipped through Cathy's chart. "And the periods of crying?"

"The same. And this morning she was found wandering in the hallway."

The two men walked to the far side of the room.

"What do you think?" one doctor asked the other.

"I think it's gone beyond postpartum blues. Her withdrawal is almost catatonic. You say she's just given her baby up?"

"Four days ago."

"I'd better talk to the aunt. I think we should hold her for observation in Two-East for a while. She may be obsessed by feelings of guilt about the adoption. We can't take any chances on what she might do."

"You're the psychiatrist, Al."

In the weeks that followed, Cathy hardly knew who she was, or where she was, or why. Her entire existence seemed to center around the medication she received three times a day, at eight in the morning, one in the afternoon, and again at six in the evening.

To her, life was seeing everything as soft gray through listless eyes. Everything she touched seemed larger than it looked, and at times she felt as though she were floating in some strange, nebulous world—but it was a peaceful world at least.

And then one day she found herself sitting across from Holly in the day room in Two-East, found herself wondering why they were sitting there in that strange place, found that her mouth felt like it was full of cotton; her head, light with confusion.

So began the daily psychotherapy visits, the slow interest in her appearance, the gradual decrease in medication.

The staff at Two-East had succeeded in cracking open the cocoon her mind had built around her body, succeeded in letting the light into her self-imposed dark world, succeeded in coaxing her out into the sunshine and roses of the real world.

"It's not going to be easy for you, Catherine," the therapist told her the day she was discharged, "but you have strengths that are going to get you through this period. Dr. Bernard has left a prescription for you that he wants you to take for a while. It's a mild tranquilizer, and it's important that you take it. You've been getting stronger doses here, and if you just stop cold turkey, you could have a severe reaction. Good luck, and I'll see you next week. Okay?''

"Okay," Cathy mumbled in her sleep, "everything will be okay if I just don't think about it."

But during the early hours of morning, her thoughts still zoomed in and out of past memories, faces darted at her in her dreams: Jed, lying with her on the riverbank; the helpless face of the baby boy lying against her breasts; and Steve's anguish as he blurted out, "How could you know what it's like to lose a son?"

Long before dawn, Cathy awoke, exhausted from the night's recapitulations. She rose, dressed quietly, and slipped away before Steve had awakened.

Somehow, she managed to get through the day, avoiding him whenever possible, thankful that he must have decided to give her time before pressing her for personal conversation.

Steve looked for her at noon but was told that she had left the studio. At six-thirty he parked himself in her office, waiting for her to pick up her attaché case before leaving.

Not too surprised at finding him there, she began shop talk. "Steve, Holly is about to flip out. You know the rewrite she did on the scripts for next Monday's shooting. Well all hundred and fifty freshly mimeographed copies are lost. Gone. And have you read the study by the National Institutes of Health? Says that some people think of soaps as real, use them in family interrelationships as guides for living...complains that the birthrate on soap operas is eight times as high as the national average.''

Steve watched silently as Cathy rambled on, obviously trying to avoid giving him the chance to talk about what he wanted to talk about.

"Last time we lost scripts, Cathy, they were mixed up with the supplies delivered to commissary. I'll check in the morning." Seeing her lock her filing cabinet, he reached for her attaché case. "How about sharing a cab home?" he asked, uncertain of her plans.

"Fine."

He looked relieved.

Both of them were glad the cab driver had a knack of carrying on a conversation by himself, spouting words of wisdom and a few others regarding the mayor of New York, whom he referred to as the Mayatollah.

Cathy heard Steve push the bolt in place but said nothing.

"How about a drink?" he asked casually.

"Thanks, Steve, but I don't have time."

She went upstairs, leaving him repeating to himself, "I don't have time."

After tossing his jacket and tie on a chair, he filled the ice bucket and fixed himself a drink—a stiff one.

When Cathy did come downstairs, she was carrying one of her suitcases.

A quick swallow. He hadn't been ready for that. Seeing her go back up, he added another shot of vodka to his drink and sat down facing the staircase.

Down she came with another suitcase and her makeup case. Up again and back down with her dress bag.

"Heavy date?" he asked with little emotion.

"I took a room at the Berkshire Place Hotel, Steve."

"The Berkshire? What'd you do. . .rob a bank for lunch?"

"No. I checked in. It'll be convenient."

"Convenient," he repeated dryly.

"Yes, only a few blocks from the studio. I can walk to work...no more cab fares."

"I'd have loaned you the money."

She laid her new heavy winter coat across one of the pieces of luggage. "We gave it a try, Steve, and it didn't work out."

He smiled. "And I thought we were another Romeo and Juliet...Dante and Beatrice...Sodom and Gomorrah."

She didn't smile. "I'm going to call a cab."

"I'll fix you a drink."

"I won't have time."

"Right now everyone in New York wants a cab. You'll have a half hour—minimum."

He got up and went to the bar cart. She went to the study. Returning, she admitted, "Half hour...you were right."

"Here."

She took the vodka and tonic and sat down on the sofa.

"The Berkshire's going to cost you a pretty penny, C.A."

"Just until I find an apartment. Holly's sister had one in a brownstone on the West Side. She's going to check around for me."

Steve filled his glass. "Does Devlin know you're leaving the nest?" His tone was insinuating.

"No. I only told Holly." She glanced at her wristwatch.

Sitting down, Steve stretched his legs and slid his hands in his pockets. "Did you get a suite?"

"You're funny," she said, smirking. "The room's a little smaller than your dining room."

"Kitchen privileges?"

"Room service."

"Ouch! More bucks."

"I plan on having a lot of meals at Holly's."

"And more Chinese?"

"I told you, Steve, I don't like Chinese food."

"Neither do I...now."

She knew he was referring to the dinner she had had with Devlin, but she refused to be baited by him.

"Going to be awfully quiet around here with you gone, C.A."

"Ever think about getting another roommate?" she asked, trying to be whimsical.

"No, one was enough." He tossed down half his drink. "Actually, I'm thinking about becoming a womanizer. You know, just laugh, say hi!, no involvements, no regrets."

"That should keep you busy. New York's filled with women who like that."

Cathy checked her watch again, and then, remembering something, she reached inside her purse and laid the key he had given her on the table next to her chair. She didn't see the look of sadness that filled his eyes as he watched her put it there.

"Thanks for the loan of this, Steve."

"Why don't you hold on to it?"

"And if your place is burglarized?" She tried to smile.

"The police would never know you had a key...my lips would be sealed." He couldn't smile.

An unnerving silence.

"Cathy—" "Steve—" They both spoke at once.

"Ladies first."

"Steve, I hope this isn't going to affect our work. We do work well together. I can see things shaping up already. And now with Holly here—"

"Of course it won't. Why should it?"

"Good. I didn't think it would, but I wanted to hear you say it."

Another silence, during which Cathy tried to avoid his stare, tried not to notice the sullen arch of his mouth, the little uplift of one nostril—as though he smelled something rotten.

"Well!" he said a little too emphatically, trying to find something to say, "they say a man's home is his castle. Why is it that suddenly it feels like my prison?"

Cathy checked her watch.

"Don't worry, C.A., when the cab gets here it'll sound like Gabriel blowing his brains out on his horn."

He checked her almost untouched drink and fixed himself another.

"Let's see," he asked, "what were we going to have for dinner tonight?"

"You were going to barbecue steaks on the deck. She thought a moment. "But I forgot to take the steaks out of the freezer." Another thought. "There's some lasagna left. You could stick it in the microwave."

"No," he said colorlessly.

Suddenly the whole house seemed to vibrate with the sound of the taxi's horn. They were both startled, not so much by the jarring blare, but because they both knew the time had arrived to say good-bye, and Cathy hated good-byes—she detested them.

Quickly Steve put his glass down. "Cathy!"

She stood up. "Will you help me, Steve?"

She didn't want him to say anything. She just wanted to get in the cab and leave—leave him, leave his home, leave the sick feeling she had in the pit of her stomach; leave before the tears came that she felt forming on her eyelids.

"I love you, Cathy. Don't leave...please don't."

Another blare of the horn, this time more furious.

"He's waiting. I've got to go."

"Forget it! Cathy, I can't let you walk out like this!"

"I'm going, Steve. I—"

His lips were on hers before she could object. His mouth ground on hers with a fury that frightened her. Hearing yet another and longer impatient blare, she pushed him away, grabbed one suitcase and ran from the room.

The taxi was about to pull away as she reached the street. Seeing Steve coming, carrying the rest of her luggage, the driver got out and opened the trunk, and in another minute he pulled away from the curb, leaving Cathy's eyes imprinted with the picture of Steve standing on the sidewalk, looking like a man who had succumbed to hopelessness.

In his rearview mirror, the driver caught a glimpse of the woman behind him and watched her dab at her eyes with a small handkerchief. He decided conversation was not the thing she needed right now.

What she needed, she had just left standing alone on a sidewalk in the Village.

Chapter Eleven

In the days that followed, Cathy became adjusted to her room at the Berkshire, to breakfast at a nearby fast-food chain. For all of Holly's prodding she had yet to have dinner with her at her sister's. Many a night she had simply skipped eating, taking work home with her to the too-quiet room at the hotel.

She had almost, but not quite, become used to the silence as she worked on projected story ideas, schedules, the budget; and so she was surprised when one evening around seven-thirty, after she had just settled down to go over some proposed scripts Holly had drafted, she heard a knock on the door to her room.

"Yes?" she called before opening the door.

"Delivery!" The voice that answered was high-pitched and unnatural.

Opening the door, Cathy found Steve, a plaid blanket strewn over one arm, a small silver vase with a yellow rose in his other hand. Quickly he stepped inside, ignoring the surprised look on her face.

"Brought you a house-warming present." He looked around the bedroom. "Humph...even has a window."

"What are you doing here, Steve?" she asked, not too warmly, but feeling good inside.

He held up the rose for her to sniff. "Gotta take time to smell the roses."

"Thank you." She set it down on the dresser and then eyed the blanket suspiciously. "Not thinking of camping here, I hope."

"You'd have to pay extra...don't you know anything about hotel rules?"

"Steve, I have work to do."

"So do I. Holly says you've lost at least five pounds." He examined her from head to toe and then back up again. "Seems like my life's work is to make sure you eat something. Well, they say it's easier to put it on than take off." He looked at the white dress she was wearing. "Do you have something you could slip into that's not white?"

"What's wrong with this dress?" she asked, annoyed.

"It's white."

"I *know* it's white."

"Trust me. Put something else on."

"Steve!"

"Cathy, if you don't, I will scream. I can just see the headlines tomorrow...executive producer tells of night of terror after being lured to the bedroom of sex-crazed female."

"You would, too!" She thought a moment, looking at his casual outfit—jeans and T-shirt. "What am I dressing for, the Bronx Zoo?"

"Just don't overdress or I'll feel embarrassed being with you." He plunked himself in the one easy chair.

Opening the closet door, Cathy turned, looked at his clothes again, and then selected a striped tank top and navy chambray pants. Then, sarcastically, she quipped, "At least if we look like we're together, we might get the same cell."

Before taking her clothes into the bathroom to change, she tossed the folder holding her proposed plot ideas at him. "Here, see what you think about these."

"Work...is that all you ever think about?"

"Someone has to."

The bathroom door closed a little too defiantly, and minutes later she was back.

"My, my...you have lost weight. Ever think of writing a book?"

"That's just what the world needs," she answered curtly, "another book on how to lose weight."

She dropped her hotel key into her purse.

"Aren't you going to wear your rose? This is a special celebration this evening." He sounded stunned that she shouldn't have thought of it.

"What celebration?"

"Our anniversary."

"What anniversary?"

"Of our one-week trial separation." His fingers roamed across his forehead in mock exasperation. "Must I remind you of *everything*?"

"Steve, there is nothing *trial* about our separation, and don't start that again, please."

"If you put the rose on."

"Okay, okay. I'll put the rose on."

She searched for a pin in her sewing kit and attached the rose to her red-and-white tank top. Looking in the mirror, she teased, "You'll excuse the white in my top. I don't have a complete wardrobe of dining-out apparel."

The doorman didn't look twice at the colorful couple that sauntered onto Fifty-second Street. As they headed for the curb, he automatically hailed a cab that seemed to be waiting for them.

Cathy overheard Steve give the driver a Broadway address.

"Where are we dining, Steve. . .Nedick's?"

"Oh, so you've broadened your culinary experience since you left home."

"Ha, ha. . .I didn't *leave home*."

"Well, more about that later," he mumbled to himself.

The rhythmic tapping of his fingers against his leg caught her attention. Then, looking up at him, she saw that he was eyeing her with that enigmatic gaze of his.

"You've got the look of a lecher, Steve. By the way, how's your womanizing coming along?"

"Does Macy's talk to Gimbels?"

When the taxi stopped on Broadway, Steve told Cathy to wait in the cab. Watching the meter, she began to get nervous when almost five minutes passed.

Steve hopped back in and directed the cabby again, but Cathy was too interested in something else to hear where. Her eyes were glued to the shopping bag which smelled like an East European delicatessen.

She was even more surprised when he later all but dragged her and the shopping bag from the taxi and hurried her deep into Central Park.

Night was descending and she had heard all the savage stories of Central Park at night, but she felt a little more at ease at seeing so many people wandering about.

"Steve, do we have to run?" she complained.

"We're late...c'mon...move it."

He told her their destination was the Great Lawn—wherever that was—but as he slowed down she could hear music and singing filtering through the trees.

And then, quite a distance away, Cathy saw a bandshell, a symphony orchestra, and singers dressed in evening clothes; she heard what she knew to be *La Traviata*.

At the outskirts of the thousand or so people nestled on blankets dotted with picnic baskets, Steve spread his plaid blanket down on the grass. "Good, we didn't miss it."

"Miss what?" she asked, watching him dip into the bag to retrieve a bottle of wine and two paper cups.

"The *Libiamo*...the drinking duet," he said quickly, handing her the two cups and then pouring the wine.

"Do we take our cue from them, or can I try this now?" she asked innocently.

Looking at her disappointingly, he sighed, "Really, Cathy, have you no soul?"

She waited. As the orchestra began the soft, waltzlike oom-pah-pah, Steve lifted his paper cup and waited for her to do likewise.

"*Cin-cin*, C.A."

As Steve put the cup to his lips, his eyes peered over the paper rim, feasting on her, shining like newborn stars taking in their first view of the universe.

Cathy's pulse quickened. Her lips parted to sip her wine, but her brain forgot to tell her hand to lift it to her mouth, so immersed was she in the wonderment of the eyes that held hers fast, those eyes with the fire behind them, a fire fueled by passion.

"*Cin-cin*," she answered, watching him lower his cup.

And now her eyes fixed on his wine-moistened mouth, on those lips that had kissed her so tenderly, so fiercely, that had yelled at her, had whispered so many endearments.

The change of voice from tenor to soprano brought her back from her tangential thoughts as Steve lay back on the blanket, eyes closed, his arm under his head, obviously enjoying the music. Cathy enjoyed it, too, but her eyes were open, and on Steve.

She smiled at his "I love New York" T-shirt, and then her glance swept down to the hand across his waist. The thought that even his fingernails were beautiful struck her as odd. His hand and arm were powerful, but at the same time they were beautiful to her. Even in the careless light of the park his tanned skin shone and the brownish sweeps of fine hair begged to be disturbed.

Then she took in the tightness of his jeans, her heart beating a little faster. Down her eyes went, still farther, to those god-awful sneakers that she had secretly threatened to discard, but had never dared to.

Once again she watched the silent undulation of his chest, remembering how, in the quiet hours of night, she had lain beside him, running her fingertips across it, moving upward to his strong neck, and upward still to caress his cheek as he slept.

In the soft half-light, his features somehow seemed sharper, stronger, more clearly defined. She imagined her fingers stroking his forehead, that little scar, running across the manly symmetry of his brows and the long, dark lashes that hovered underneath them. But it wasn't her fingers she imagined on his mouth—it was her lips that she wanted there.

Cathy leaned back on the blanket, resting on her elbows, listening to the soprano sing of her doubts about her new love. What was it Steve had said earlier—a trial separation?

To her it was a trial all right, but that wasn't what he had meant—at least she didn't think so. And then she decided that in the week they had lived apart, this was the first moment that she truly felt relaxed, that she could take each breath without that dull pain in her chest, without that feeling that she was about to cry at any moment.

Steve sat up, his attention on the roulades the soprano was effortlessly spinning out. At the end of the first act, he added his frenetic applause to that of the enthusiastic crowd in the park.

"Man, if that doesn't give you an appetite, nothing will," he told her, again dipping into the magical deli bag.

In moments, he made her the biggest and fattest pastrami-and-cheese sandwich on rye that she had ever seen.

"Steve, this is enough for both of us," Cathy protested.

He was busy chewing, but between chews he managed a muffled, "Don't get too full. We've got stuffed vine leaves for dessert."

"Can we wait for that until after the second act?" she pleaded.

"Okay. I can nibble on the smoked beef jerky."

There wasn't a doubt in Cathy's mind that somewhere in that bag he did have smoked beef jerky.

As Violetta died at the end of the opera, Cathy thought she, too, was going to die, but not from consumption—from overeating.

Steve had insisted she finish the entire sandwich, which she tried to tell him was equivalent to a loaf of bread and at least half a cow, not to mention the wheel of cheese—the stuffed vine leaf, and the smoked beef jerky she had valiantly tried to gnaw on without much success.

Following the mob onto Fifth Avenue, he suggested they walk a few blocks, for which she was extremely grateful.

Leisurely they walked hand in hand, she with her free hand in her pocket; he, swinging the remnants of food in the bag, whistling themes from *La Traviata*.

Steve's hand felt warm in Cathy's, and to her it seemed like ages since she had last touched him—and it seemed so right for her hand to be in his.

They walked quietly, each involved in private thoughts. Cathy wondered if Steve was thinking of her as she was thinking of him, but at the sight of their approaching Rockefeller Center, her heart almost stopped. They were almost at the hotel and would be saying good night.

Turning on Fifty-second Street, Steve stopped.

"Another memory evening for me, Cathy. Thanks."

"Thank you, Steve...it was beautiful, except for the beef jerky," she added, trying desperately to be cheerful.

"Cathy. . ."—his eyes pleaded—"ready to come home?"

God, how she wanted to say yes! The thought of going back up to her little room alone was horrifying, but the thought of retracing her life to that night they both sat waiting for the cab to take her away from him was even more distressful.

"No, Steve…I'm not," she said quietly, looking away from him.

"Oh," was all he could say softly. Then, "Well…see you tomorrow at the studio. How about lunch?"

"Already scheduled with Holly and Vanessa. We're going to gang up on her before she reads the new scripts…if they ever deliver them."

"They will."

"You sound pretty sure about that."

"Trust me," he said, but there was something in his voice that made her think he wasn't only talking about the scripts.

"I do trust you, Steve." Then, looking into his eyes, she said, "I trust you not to make this any harder for me than it already is." She kissed his cheek. "Good night, Steve…and thanks again." She walked hurriedly toward the hotel, leaving Steve on the street with his shopping bag.

Alone in her room, Cathy looked around at the four walls of her new *home*. Suddenly it seemed to her that the walls were closing in on her, threatening to suffocate her. Her head ached, her breaths came in quick, shallow puffs. Not knowing why, she went to the little desk littered with scripts and work papers, and with one furious sweep sent them flying across the room.

Seconds later she was kneeling on the floor retrieving them, trying to make order out of the disarray of papers and folders. She sank back on her ankles and let her tears wash away the tightness of her lids.

Unpinning the wilted yellow rose from her top, she held it to her lips, wondering what she had done in life that made loving someone so miserable for her.

Chapter Twelve

The taping day at "Search for Love" began in the pre-dawn hours when the crew came in to assemble the sets needed for the day's schedule. Between eight-thirty and nine, cast members would straggle into the rehearsal room for blocking sessions with the director. With tables and chairs serving as furniture markers, the actors would walk through their scenes, reciting their lines and miming the actions they would perform in the scene they were rehearsing, whether it was drinking a drink made of colored water or making passionate love in bed, and after the initial walk-through, there would be two more rehearsals on the set before the taping actually began—the second run-through done in costume.

Cathy had already spent some time in her office when she walked into the rehearsal room; she was surprised to see that several cast members were already there, among them, Ted and Vanessa.

The two of them were poring over their scripts, and from the looks on their faces Cathy immediately guessed that, as Steve had said they would be, the scripts had been delivered and had been distributed to those present.

One look at Ted's red socks made Cathy wonder if that was the only color he bought or if that was the only pair he had. Catching sight of her, he looked up and slapped the script with his hand.

"A coma! You've got to be kidding. My fans will hit the roof!"

"Let the powers-that-be worry about that, Ted," she said firmly, casually tossing her clipboard onto the coffee table as she poured herself a cup. "Besides, you've got a chance to do some real acting...with your mouth shut."

"Oh yeah?"

"Yeah," she repeated, mimicking his tone. "Morning, Vanessa," she said cheerfully, but Vanessa was so engrossed flipping through her scenes, she never heard her.

"Listen here, Miss Arensen—" Ted began.

"Catherine the Great to you, Ted."

He sputtered, but before he could get a word out, Cathy moved next to him, leaning against the long wooden table.

"Ted, have you ever seen the movie *Johnny Belinda?*"

The look on his face told her he had no idea of what she was talking about.

"Well, Ted, in the movie, Jane Wyman plays a deaf-mute. She didn't say a word, Ted, not a word, and if my memory serves me correctly, she won an Academy Award for her performance."

Cathy could almost hear the rusty wheels turning in that vacant space between his handsome ears.

"She didn't say a word?" he asked suspiciously.

"Not a word, Ted."

"And she got an Academy Award for that?"

"An Oscar."

"How 'bout that!"

"Ted"—she placed her hand on his muscular shoulder—"this could be your springboard to Hollywood." *Would to God,* she added mentally.

"And to an Oscar," he added happily.

One down, Cathy thought, *and now for Vanessa.* She took a seat next to her. Vanessa, like Ted, was wide-eyed.

"How's it going?" Cathy asked, trying to sound casual.

"Cathy...have you seen this?" She held her script up, her mouth hanging open.

"Yes. Holly and I worked on it together. Why?"

"This makes it sound like I'm falling in love with Devlin."

"I know, and you do."

"But he's so much younger than Ted."

"That's the idea."

"But look." She flipped over some pages. "Here...I go to a mirror and start examining my face...looking for wrinkles."

"I do that every morning, Vanessa. That's a very natural act for a woman, especially a woman in love with a younger man."

"A younger man! Is the story going to make that very obvious?" Terror filled her green eyes.

"It will allude to it, but we won't run it into the ground. More important is to show the audience you are capable of falling in love and being hurt when it doesn't work out."

Vanessa just stared at Cathy for a moment. Then: "But Cathy, I've played a bitch for thirteen years...and successfully. It's my meal ticket, the only ticket I've ever had. If you tear it up—"

"No one is going to do that," Cathy assured her. "We're just going to give you a transfer to another line for a while. Yes, you're going to fall in love, be dropped by—"

"Dropped!"

"...but then you're going to put your armor on and get even, in your own inimitable style. Okay?"

"Cathy, I don't know about all this," she said dubiously.

Just then, Steve stuck his head in the door to the rehearsal room and beckoned to Cathy.

"Listen, Vanessa, I've got to run, but I want you to have lunch with Holly and me and we'll talk it out. At one o'clock, okay?"

Still in shock, Vanessa nodded and Cathy went to see what Steve wanted.

"What's with Vanessa?" he asked curiously.

"Just temporary script shock, but she'll come through it." Looking back at Vanessa, she added, "She's a great gal, though." Then, to Steve, she said, "Now what was the come-hither finger for?"

"We've got problems." He handed her a sheet of paper.

"We have no problems," she said hopefully. Scanning the paper: "We've got problems."

Steve leaned back against the wall in the corridor. "The July sweeps were bad enough according to the Nielsens and the Arbitron ratings, and the VP of daytime programming just handed me this for August. It should have a black border around it.''

Cathy reread the latest ratings. ''Doesn't he realize the ratings aren't going to change overnight? Did you tell him we were pinpointing the weak and strong spots, and that our stories would climax during the November sweeps period?''

''That and more. I guaranteed him that 'SFL' would be back in the top five soaps again before Christmas.''

''What did he say?''

''That if it wasn't, Christmas would be a cold time for the you-know-what to hit the fan.''

''Well, there's not much else that can happen today,'' she said, not realizing that she would be sorry for that statement.

It was a little after six o'clock when Steve burst into her office. ''Have you heard?''

''Heard what?''

''About the blackout?''

''What blackout?''

''There's a twenty-block blackout on the East Side, just around the garment district...something about a burned-out power substation.''

''So?'' she said, not understanding why he was sounding so uptight, yet smiling.

''The Berkshire is in the middle of it, Cathy.''

She put her selected folders in her case and closed it. ''So the lights will be off for a few hours.''

''A few hours! Have you been down a manhole in New York lately? Con Ed's got a million miles of wiring down there. It could take them a week to even find the problem.''

Suspiciously, she repeated, ''A week?''

"The candlelight would be romantic in that room of yours, but not very practical...or safe."

"Steve, I would certainly be safe at the Berkshire."

"You'll probably find this hard to believe, Cathy, but there are some pretty strange men in this town."

She eyed him knowingly. "Tell me about it."

"I mean *strange,* and they don't just settle for playing footsie when the lights go out." He took her case from the desk. "Come on. You're coming home with me."

"Just like that."

"Just like this!" He picked up her handbag also, and then he pulled her from the office.

Resisting all the way down the elevator, Cathy finally agreed to spend one night at his house if they would stop by her hotel room to pick up the basic necessities of life.

When the taxi pulled up in front of the house on St. Luke's Place, Cathy felt her heart skip a beat. Her first impulse was to kiss the cab driver, but his big cigar made her think twice about that.

Carrying her one suitcase inside, Steve let her carry the precious makeup case. When she walked into her bedroom she felt that for the first time she really knew the meaning of the word *home*.

As she placed her suitcase on the bed, she noted the smile of self-satisfaction on Steve's face, and it crossed her mind that he would be capable of putting a twenty-block stretch of Manhattan in the dark.

"Now then, get comfortable. Cocktails in fifteen minutes." He turned to leave, but at the door he stopped, turned again, and put one arm against the doorframe. "I must be blessed with great prescience."

"Why?"

"I stocked up on groceries yesterday, and I wasn't even thinking about that appetite of yours." As he went down the hall to his room, Cathy heard him whistling.

"Well, Catherine"—she began to talk to herself—"here we are. . .back in never-never land."

Exactly fifteen minutes later Cathy had changed out of her work clothes and was downstairs in the livng room. She heard Steve puttering in the kitchen and then he appeared in the doorway.

"How about fixing the drinks. . .ice is in the bucket."

As she was about to lift the lid to the ice bucket, she noticed a white envelope taped to the handle of the bar cart. Lifting it she read, *Cathy's key*.

A happy warmth spread through her as she put ice in the glasses—a warmth her heart hadn't felt for weeks.

"Need any help?" she asked from the living room.

"No. Why don't you put something on the stereo?"

She glanced through his collection of cassettes, trying to remember the tape he had played the first night she was there. A Rachmaninoff symphony, she recalled. Then, finding it, she saw it was cued up for the adagio on side two.

As the strings began their rolling, lush melody, Steve called from the kitchen. "Louder!"

Cathy turned the volume up and the music filled the house—and probably half the Village, she thought.

Sipping her drink, she looked around the familiar room, at the sofa and matching easy chairs, the marble end tables, the fireplace with its huge mirror. Then, walking to it, she ran her fingers across his football trophy and found herself thinking she was happy he had stopped playing the game— one scar, little as it was, was enough.

Again from the kitchen: "Boy, those Russians are a passionate lot, aren't they?"

Cathy sat on the sofa, kicked her sandals off, and curled her legs under her. "Are you Russian, Steve?"

"Somewhere there's a little."

"That figures," she said, smiling to herself.

He appeared at the door, a large spoon in one hand. "And what's that supposed to mean?"

"Nothing...just making conversation."

"Oh. I was hoping it was a compliment." He disappeared and then reappeared. "Pork chops baked in milk okay?"

"Sounds delicous. Make sure they're done, though," she warned.

"Listen, anyone who dines at Nedick's!...Need I say more?"

"Want your drink in there?"

"No, I'll be right out, just another minute."

Cathy leaned back on the sofa, feeling as though the music was flowing right through her body. She recalled Steve's calling his home a prison when she was leaving, and it seemed to her that her hotel room had been a prison of sorts. And now, sitting there, knowing he was so close, she felt that all was right with the world once again.

Catching sight of Steve coming in, she straightened up and watched him shrug his shoulders, his palms lifted, as he said breezily, "The rest is in the hands of the big chef in the sky."

She pointed to the table across the room. "I put your drink over there."

He looked at the empty chair next to the table, over at Cathy, and then back to the chair. Getting his drink, he said,

"I like it better over here," as he sat down on the floor in front of the sofa, his back leaning against it.

"*Cin-cin,* C.A."

"*Cin-cin,* she replied, letting him clink his glass against hers.

"Oh, that's good," he sighed taking a sip. "It's been quite a day."

"I'm afraid to say nothing else can happen," she added.

He looked up at her. "Nothing we couldn't handle...together."

The look in his eyes and the suggestion of a smile on his face alerted her. She decided to talk about work.

"Steve, as one producer to another—"

"Cathy, we've put in our share of work for the day," he said seriously. "Let's have some personal time now...time just for us."

She wasn't to be deterred. "I love my work, Steve...it's my vocation as well as my avocation."

"Love it? I saw you in the studio tearing those feathers from Vanessa's outfit."

"Steve, what is it with wardrobe?" she asked in exasperation. "Do you have any idea how many birds had to die to make that outfit? She had feathers sticking out all over her...even in that dumb turban. She looked like a white peacock in heat."

He laughed. "So now you're an expert in ornithology."

Leaning his head back, glancing up at her, he declared, "You're something else, C.A."

Cathy had missed being called by her initials, something Steve never did in the office—his "C.A." and her "S.B." were something they shared between them, something that was theirs alone.

Still looking up at her, Steve told her, "You're good at your job. You manage things and you lead people, and you emphasize leadership, not management. That's good."

"You do a pretty good job yourself, S.B."

"You're right," he said quickly, but then thinking of the downturn "SFL" had taken in the ratings the past year, "with the exception of my recent lull."

"Don't you know why?" she asked seriously.

He smiled mischievously. "Would you buy. . .traumatic toilet training as the cause?"

There he was again, she decided, forcing humor to cover up the pain she now realized was gnawing at his insides—a feeling of guilt that would give him no peace.

"No, Steve, I wouldn't, and I don't think it's good for you not to recognize openly what the problem's been."

"The psychiatrist is in," he said officiously.

"I'm not getting psychiatric on you. I just worry about you, that's all."

He angled his body and rested his elbow on the sofa, his chin resting in his palm. "That's sweet, Cathy," he said softly. I worry about you, too. That must mean something."

Taking his empty glass and hers to the bar cart, she explained, "It means we're a couple of worrywarts, that's what it means."

He stretched his legs out and crossed them at the ankles. "What do you suggest we do about that?" His tone was measured, quizzical.

Looking down at him from across the room, she queried, "What do you mean?"

He folded his arms across his chest. "Well, with you living in midtown and me down here, it's just going to add a lot more worrying for both uf us...right?"

She went back to mixing his drink. "I'd do a lot more worrying living here."

"Now," said he curiously, "what do *you* mean?"

Pouring the tonic, she said, "I mean we've been through this before. Change the subject."

He raised his knees and spread his arms across them. "I can't. . .it's all I think of day and night, but particularly during the night."

She handed him the drink and took a seat in the chair across from him, not wanting to say what she knew she would say if he pressed her.

"What would worry you about coming home again, Cathy?" A thunderous silence. "A minute ago you told me I had to recognize my problem openly. What's yours?" He wondered why she wouldn't look at him. "Why is it I keep thinking you're hiding something?"

If only she hadn't quit smoking, she thought. She could light a cigarette now—that would give her something to do to stall, to keep the words that were gagging in her throat from coming to her lips.

"Well, C.A.?" he asked again, "what worries you so about living here?"

Absently, her fingers turned her glass on the napkin on the marble-topped table, and although she fought it, she heard herself say, "I don't want to fall in love with you again, Steve."

"Ah. . .so you're cured now." He placed his palms behind his head and leaned backward. "Yes, being in love is a very serious condition...lots of side effects. Sleepless nights?'' he asked.

"Yes."

"No appetite?"

"Yes."

"Feel like crying sometimes?"

"Yes."

"That's it...you had it. Glad you got over it. Hope I will soon. It's about as much fun as having shingles."

Still twisting her glass: "Your pork chops are going to burn."

He looked at his watch. "No way. I know what I'm doing."

"Do you?" she asked seriously.

"I think so."

"How well do you really know me, Steve? How much do you know about Catherine Arensen?"

"All that I need to...unless you're an alien being who's come to rape and pillage Manhattan's finest."

She laughed, more from nervousness than anything else.

"Cathy, please come back. I miss you something awful."

As she leaned her elbow on the arm of the chair and let her fingers slip up against the side of her forehead, her loose hair fell against her arm. Suddenly she felt her heart grow stronger, gaining strength over her confused reason. It would be so easy just to say yes.

"I want to, Steve. I've missed being here with you, but—"

He jumped up. "Good! That's settled. We'll pick up the rest of your things tomorrow."

"No, it's not settled! You're rushing me again."

He sat back down quickly and raised the palms of his hands in defense. "Sorry."

She looked over at him as he sat there, arms across his raised knees, hands clasped, waiting for her to say something. The more he waited, the more she knew she had to decide. The war inside her was on again—brain against heart, and it seemed to be an evenly matched battle, until she saw the corners of his mouth arch upward a little, until she saw his warm brown eyes begin to glisten, until she saw him cock his head slightly as he stared at her in his own affectionate way. And then she knew the war was over: her heart, singing victoriously, told her so.

"If I do...*if*...there've got to be certain conditions, and I mean it, Steve."

"No hanky-panky," he said.

"Right."

"No declarations of love."

"Right."

"No foolin' around in the hot tub."

"Right."

"No short brown robe."

"Definitely right!" she agreed.

"Well, so much for my wild life as a bachelor."

Now Cathy jumped up. "You're doing it again, Steve!"

Confused, he looked up at her. "Doing what?"

"Hiding your feelings behind those smart remarks of yours, that's what."

Silently, he ran his fingers through his hair and sighed deeply, knowing that she was speaking the truth and admiring her for having the courage to speak it. Then, he looked over at her with pleading eyes. "I could change for you...if you'll help me."

Sitting on the sofa next to him, she stroked his head. "I don't want you to change for me, Steve. I want you to change for yourself. I don't want you making promises you don't think you can really keep."

He reached for her hand and kissed her palm, sending that now familiar thrill rushing up her arm.

"We all need someone, Cathy...someone special like you."

The timer went off in the kitchen, not a second too soon, she thought.

All through dinner and the rest of the evening, Cathy realized she had made the right decision: life again took on a relaxed beauty, a beauty she had sorely missed, and the light in her heart came on three days before the lights in midtown Manhattan.

In the weeks that followed, the pact that she and Steve made held securely, each of them directing their frustrated energies into "Search for Love." The ratings began a slow ascent in the charts, their polished programs highlighting a double wedding, a costumed ball, young love, middle-aged romance; and Holly's gift for words proved that even love among the elderly could grab the attention of a youthful audience.

And Vanessa—well, she more than proved herself the actress Cathy knew she could be in her disastrous on-camera affair with Devlin; and as Cathy had predicted, "SFL's" fan mail—even from the wife of the VP of day-time programming—shot up every time Devlin disrobed for the camera and flashed those violet-blues of his.

But in October an unexpected disaster hit St. Luke's Place: Steve's Oktoberfest celebration. For a week he faithfully turned a gorgeous piece of beef in his personally concocted marinade, a mixture loaded with the bock beer he had hoarded since spring. Only God knew what else he had put in that marinade, and Cathy certainly didn't want to know, but her trips to the refrigerator became fewer and fewer and faster and faster to avoid smelling what he said would be sauerbraten.

By the fifth day the smell filled the house, her clothes closet, and, she was afraid, even her hair—no matter how often she shampooed it. But Steve was ecstatic, proclaiming it would be a meal she would not soon forget.

The day of celebration arrived, and by that time the odor had so dazed Cathy that her eyes resembled the spiral walkway at the Guggenheim Museum.

Even an extra cocktail failed to help prepare her for the aroma that steamed up from the platter he proudly laid on the dining-room table. The boiled potatoes had a funny color, as did the boiled cabbage. He confessed that perhaps he had put too much bock beer in the cooking water.

Mercifully, Cathy was spared having to taste anything, for after one forkful of the sauerbraten, Steve packaged the meal in aluminum foil, tossed it, and quietly escorted Cathy out for dinner.

But the odor lingered on, and it was not until after Santa arrived at Macy's in his annual Thanksgiving Day Parade, after the air had turned cool and every window had been opened, that Cathy could fall asleep at night without covering her nostrils with her hand.

Steve had threatened a Thanksgiving spread for Holly and her sister, but Cathy's report of what became known as his "Oktoberbust" prodded Holly to invite them instead.

And then came the cold winds from Canada, bringing with them the first heavy snow of winter. At first, Cathy thought the ten-plus inches that had fallen was delightful, and in parts of the Village it was: the narrow streets with their old houses and lampposts drenched in the snow's soft whiteness had a Christmas-card charm about them, but midtown Manhattan was turned into a wild and bewildering waste of slush and ice, disrupting the city's transportation, almost paralyzing the busy thoroughfares, causing bottlenecks on surrounding highways, bridges, and already overcrowded expressways. The sky over Manhattan, however, was beautiful—an intense blue with few clouds, a crystalline clarity pervading the canopy over the little island.

With the first heavy snow also came the first snowman that Cathy had built in more than fifteen years. He stood tall and proud and fat in the little garden outside the living room, sporting one of Steve's striped scarfs and crowned with his green tennis visor, a plunger regally stuck through his armpit.

It was with a strange kind of sorrow that she and Steve found him after work one evening. The darkness in the garden did little to make him a cheerful sight. The plunger that was his scepter, his symbol of sovereignty, lay on the ground, and Steve's tennis visor had slipped to his round shoulders, no longer supported by the half-melted head.

Chapter Thirteen

It was a few days before Christmas. A gray day. A light snow was falling.

He was walking down the street just outside Saks Fifth Avenue as Cathy came rushing out from her lunchtime shopping for Christmas presents for Holly and Vanessa. Their collision sent her packages flying onto the wet sidewalk.

"Oops!" came his laughing voice as they both bent down to retrieve her purchases.

As she rose, her eyes told her that he was wearing the uniform of an Air Force officer; reaching a standing position, his bars told her he was a captain.

"I'm sorry," she apologized, "it was my—"

As her eyes examined his face through the falling snowflakes, she had a feeling that was near to terror. It was a face she knew, except for the dark brown mustache, but there was no mistaking the bright gray eyes, the long dark eyelashes.

At the same time, the officer was studying her face.

"Catherine?" he asked suddenly, his eyes widening.

In seconds, the years slipped away for Cathy. She was seventeen again, and the crazy mixture of emotions of that time surged into her consciousness: love, hate, fear.

"Jed?"

Thinking she was about to drop her packages, his hands flew out to support them.

"It is you, Catherine! Talk about a small world. What are you doing in New York? Are your parents here? Do you live here?"

"Hold on, Jed," she pleaded. "Let me get my breath."

"Catherine, this is a miracle. I never thought I'd see you again." He took the packages she was holding.

Cathy made no objection; she was still too stunned.

"God, it's good to see you again," he said, his eyes scanning her figure, slender-looking even in the belted coat with its fox collar. He studied her face and loose-flowing hair under her fox hat. "You're more beautiful now than you were in high school," he added sincerely, his gray eyes glowing with approval.

"That was a long time ago, Jed," she said weakly.

"It could have been yesterday, now that I see you again." He looked at her gloved hand. "Are you married?"

"No," she admitted, suddenly wishing she had said yes.

"I can't believe this...running into you in the middle of New York. Listen, we've got to talk. We've got a lot to catching up to do. How about a drink?"

"No...no drink." Her mind was still reeling.

He took her arm. "You're not going to get away from me now, not just like that."

Standing in the middle of the busy sidewalk outside Saks was disconcerting to her. Looking up through the falling snow toward the next street behind him she saw the twin spires of Saint Patrick's Cathedral. Ironically, she thought, it would be an appropriate place to talk to him—of all people.

"Yes, Jed," she said, a slight bitterness creeping into her voice, "we should talk."

Still absorbing the change she had undergone from a bubbly teenager to the sophisticated and elegant woman she now was, Jed followed her across the street and up the steps of Saint Patrick's.

Inside, an unseen organ softly played Christmas carols, but even so, Cathy felt the hush, the sanctity of the towering cathedral. Jed followed her to the last pew, where they sat down.

"Have you been in the Air Force long, Jed?" she asked quietly, looking at his thick brown hair, hair now cut much shorter than when she had last seen him.

"I'm career. . .the ROTC paid off."

"Stationed near here?"

"No, in Maryland. I'm here for the holidays."

She noticed that he wore no wedding ring, but asked, anyway. "Married?"

"No."

Now she wished he had said yes.

"Catherine, was. . ." he stammered, "was there? I mean, did you—?"

"Did I have the baby?" She continued his question before he could finish asking. "Yes, I did. I told you abortion was out of the question."

He sank back in the hard seat, his nervous fingers running around the rim of the officer's emblem on his blue cap.

"You have a son, Jed," she said in a hushed voice.

"A son?" he repeated. "Can I see him, Catherine?"

"I'm afraid not, Jed. . .even if I wanted you to."

"What do you mean?"

"I gave our son up for adoption," she told him, her eyes burning at the memory.

"Adoption? Do you know where he is?"

"No, and I don't want to know," she said firmly.

At first he thought she had hardened to the situation, but looking at her, he saw the tear that moved slowly down her cheek.

"I'm sorry, Catherine. . .really sorry," he murmured. Then, after a pause: "Why didn't you keep him?"

Cathy just looked at him, her eyes clouded with contempt. "Alone, at seventeen? Remember, Jed, fourteen years ago an unwed mother was not the most socially accepted person around." She brushed the moisture from her eyes. "My father just about threw me out, in spite of my mother's pleading with him. I went to Los Angeles and stayed with my aunt."

"I see," he said quietly.

"No you don't see," she said bitterly. "True parenthood is a function of love and care, not just biology. Our son needed a mother *and* father, a stable home, and I saw to it that he got it. It wasn't his fault that we—"

"Catherine, we were so young. You were only seventeen, and I was only a year older. People make mistakes."

"Children shouldn't be mistakes, Jed, and they shouldn't have to pay for their parents' mistakes."

"Feeling that she had said what had to be said, Cathy picked up her packages. "I've got to get back to work. I wish I could say it's been nice seeing you again."

Again he took her arm. "Catherine, wait. Just another minute, please."

"Why? What's the purpose?"

"You can't just walk out of my life again."

"Aren't you somewhat confused? It was you who walked out. No, you *ran* out of my life. One day I told you I was pregnant. The next, you were gone." She looked into his gray eyes. "Where did you go?"

"Chicago," he answered meekly.

"And did you think of me often, Jed?" she asked sarcastically.

"Would you believe me if I said I did?"

"No," she answered flatly.

"Well, I did. I went back to find you."

"You looked for me?"

"I asked your father. He said he didn't know and he didn't care where you were." He paused. "Did he know that I was—"

"The father? No. I'm not sure he really cared who the father was. He was too eaten up with the fact that a daughter of his could be a tramp."

"Is that what he said?"

"Among other things."

The strains of "Silent Night" floated through the cathedral, echoing about them as they sat there together.

"Did you have a bad time, Catherine?"

"If you call a breakdown a bad time, I did."

"Are you doing okay now?" he asked, concerned.

Cathy stood up and glared down at him. "The crying at night didn't last for more than five years, Jed. After that it was a piece of cake."

She started toward the entrance and he followed.

"Catherine...wait." He caught up with her. "Listen, you've done enough penance for both of us. Can't we try to forgive ourselves now?"

She sighed deeply. "Jed, I forgave you years ago. It's just that I've tried so hard not to think about the baby I gave away, and now you're bringing the past crashing down on me again."

"Dinner. Just one lousy dinner. If we can be friends after the mess we made...I made...well, maybe it will help both of us."

"Jed, it wasn't all your fault. We messed things up together. I was too naïve, and you were too frightened."

"You're not naïve now, and I'm not frightened, and there's no way either one of us can pretend we never knew one another...that we didn't have feelings for each other." He saw her determination weaken as he spoke. "Dinner? Please?"

He smiled, and for the first time since seeing him again, Cathy realized how handsome he was, how handsome he had always been, how much she had loved him.

"All right, Jed, we'll have dinner, but if you say 'for old times' sake' just once—"

And now they both smiled, and it felt good to both of them, but particularly to Cathy. Being able to smile at him seemed to wash away some of the bitterness, some of the guilt, even, that she had harbored for so many years; it felt to her like some enormous weight was being lifted from her shoulders.

Jed took her packages and during the walk back to the studio, Cathy filled him in on what she did for a living, agreeing to meet him in the lobby at six o'clock.

At the elevator he handed her the packages, and as soon as her arms were loaded, he leaned over and kissed her lips. Cathy was taken by surprise, but his kiss brought back the clean, pungent smell of leather and the new car coat he had spread on the ground for her on that riverbank in Wisconsin.

His kiss was gentle, and when he drew back his face, she noticed that he still retained that boyish smile, that sureness of purpose—and she smiled back.

So preoccupied was she with that smile of his, Cathy didn't notice Steve watching them from across the lobby.

Upstairs in the studio, she lost no time in tracking Holly down, asking her to come to her office. She had just finished telling her of bumping into Jed, the man Holly never met but knew all about, when Steve came in.

He saw the awkward looks on both women's faces as Holly made her quick exit.

"Get all your shopping done?" he asked casually.

"Not everything. The stores are a madhouse. Next year I'm going to start in September." She moved the packages from her desk to a side table.

"Oh? Have you decided to stay in New York after your contract is up?"

Cathy thought he was acting, and sounding, strange.

"No, I haven't decided. I just meant that wherever I am, I plan to start Christmas shopping earlier."

"Be honest, C.A. Remember, we're related...brother and sister."

"And you're being relatively obscure. Be honest about what?"

"About your sudden devotion to our men in the armed forces," he answered, tugging at his earlobe.

She realized immediately that he must have seen her with Jed.

"if you mean a certain captain in the Air Force, he's an old friend. We go way back together, Steve."

"How far back?" he asked curtly, starting to lose his cool.

"I don't think that's any of your business." She opened a folder on her desk. "Now I've got work to do."

"Plotting should come easy to you."

She slammed the folder shut. "What are you talking about?"

"I'm talking about plotting! Soap women have been known to lie, cheat, commit blackmail, adultery, and even murder to get the man they want. How far are you willing to go?"

Her voice got louder. "Steve, you're being ridiculous. If you've got something to say, say it for God's sake!"

He grabbed her arm, forcing her up from her chair. "Well let God hear this! I thought that something was supposed to happen when two people shared their bodies. I thought trust was supposed to develop!"

She saw that glow in his eyes again, that fire that frightened her. She jerked her arm free.

"You belong in a loony bin, Steve! I still don't know—"

Just then, Holly stuck her head in the door. "Listen, you two, I could hear you both down the hall." She glared at

Cathy's flushed face. "Just thought you'd want to know." Quickly, she shut the door.

Steve started to leave, but turned. "You know, Cathy, if you'd open those gorgeous hazel eyes of yours, you'd be quite a woman."

He left and Cathy slumped into her chair, wondering what had gotten into him.

Later that afternoon, Steve returned to apologize and Cathy told him she was having dinner with a friend, asking him if he'd mind taking her packages home when he left. The fire started to glow in his eyes again, but Steve wrestled with his thoughts, took the packages, and slammed the door to her office as he left.

A little after six, Cathy was on her way down the elevator to meet Jed, and Holly and Steve were in conference in his office.

Steve's secretary stuck her head in the door to say good night.

"Night, Terry," he said listlessly.

"You look like you could use a drink, Steve," Holly said, examining his taut features.

"I could use a prefrontal lobotomy."

"Bad as all that, huh?"

"Worse."

"Cathy?"

"Who else?"

Holly rolled her eyes. "Oh what a tangled web love weaves for his followers," she moaned in mock seriousness. "Sounds like you two are having trouble."

"I suspected we were having trouble the time she moved out," he replied with his understated humor.

"She moved back in, didn't she?"

"But for how long? She's been seen kissing a *young, handsome* Air Force captain...on the lips...followed by a smile, yet!" He banged the top of his desk with his fist and Holly jumped.

"Easy, boy...easy. You're making the molehill grow faster than it should."

"Molehill? I'm staring up at Mount Everest!" He stood up, shoved his hands in his pockets, glanced out the window, and then turned toward Holly. "She and I even like the same kind of music."

"Oh well, that makes all the difference in the world." Then Holly said seriously, "Is that what that noisy tête-à-tête was all about this afternoon?"

"I happened to mention I knew all about her tall, dark stranger...with whom she's having dinner right now."

"*All* about him? What did she tell you?" Her words were spun out cautiously.

She piqued his curiosity. "What's to tell?"

"She didn't tell you, then," Holly concluded sadly.

For a moment Steve just looked at her, realizing she had something to say. Slipping his suit jacket on and picking up his coat, he ordered, "C'mon, Holly. You and I are going to do damage to a martini or two."

A traditional jazz pianist skittered over the keyboard in the dark bar where Steve and Holly sat. Holly related the damage that had been done some fourteen years ago when Cathy had given birth to Jed's baby. She left nothing out, telling him about the battle Cathy had gone through with anxiety and depression after giving her son up for adoption.

Steve felt himself slipping between a rock and a hard place. "I guess I've been having a bad case of tunnel vision, Holly. All I could think about was how much *I* was hurting. Poor Cathy. When I lost my son, he was gone, but she lost hers, knowing he still exists somewhere, out of reach.''

"I'd say you were acting like a normal man, Steve...but a man in love. Cathy should have been the one to tell you about Jed. If she finds out I did...oh boy.''

Steve held up two fingers, signaling for refills. "Well, I guess if the two of them have found each other again, she certainly deserves a little happiness. She's waited long enough for it.'' His frown darkened. "And now I know why Cathy's always held back from me. It's always been him,'' he concluded, feeling torn apart.

"You look like you're the one hurting now, Steve.''

He held up his index finger. "This is the only part of me that doesn't hurt.''

"What are you going to do about it?''

"Do? Nothing. What's to do?''

"Don't you think you're entitled to some happiness, too?''

"I've got 'SFL,' Holly. Thanks to you and Cathy the ratings are pushing toward heaven again. The boys upstairs are ecstatic.''

"'SFL's' not going to warm your tootsies at night.''

"So I'll get a cat.''

"Aren't you afraid of dying from a hair ball?''

"I've no intention of licking the cat to death, Holly. I've got cold feet, not a death wish.''

Holly took the olive he had put on his napkin. "I think you're throwing in the towel too hastily, Steve. I've seen the way Cathy looks at you.''

"We have a brother-sister relationship.''

"Then we're talking incest.''

As the waiter put their drinks down, he heard Holly's comment. His startled look was rewarded by her sweet smile.

Feeding her his new olive, "My, you do handle martinis well, Miss Lange."

"Seriously, Steve, if Jed were the man to make Cathy happy, he would have done it back in Wisconsin."

"He should have, but that doesn't tell me what's going on in Cathy's mind right now. No, it's got to be her decision, and I'm not going to pressure her."

"So noble."

"No...just sensible. She knows how I feel about her."

"How *do* you feel about her?"

He put his glass down and gave a low chuckle. Sometimes I could bite her right through that silky blouse of hers."

"Whew!" Holly fanned herself with her napkin. "You're giving me the vapors."

"Holly, let's run off and get married," he said jokingly.

"Oh, that would solve everything. Then there'd be four people not meant for each other."

"If I could just be sure Cathy and Jed weren't meant for each other, it would make everything so simple," he said uncertainly.

Holly reached for her coat. "Well, now that I've had my nightly proposal, I can go home and brag to my sister. I've got to go, but stay and finish your drink." She eased herself from the seat.

"Hey, does this mean we're not going Dutch?" Steve was feeling better—for the moment.

"Does the flag have fifty stars?" With her fur slung over her shoulder, Holly sauntered off, leaving him to finish his martini.

Sitting alone, Steve began making plans, tapping a toothpick on the rim of his glass, deciding how best to give Cathy the space to make her decisions. Having a tentative idea in mind, he emptied his glass and made for home.

A little after eleven o'clock, Steve was sitting in his study going over some budget figures when he heard the front door close.

"That you, Cathy?" he called.

"You were expecting Dolly Parton?"

"I should be so lucky," he mumbled. Then, out loud, "I'm in here."

Cathy walked in and nonchalantly tossed her coat on a chair; as she did she saw that he had put a picture of his ex-wife on the table next to the chair. She pretended not to notice.

"What's with the midnight oil routine?" she asked casually.

"I think, my dear, that we are going to come in on budget, that is if we stop putting toilet paper in the johns and clean the studio ourselves."

"Sounds a little drastic to me."

"Gotta watch the bucks, kiddo," he said, putting the papers in his briefcase. "How'd your evening go?"

"Fine." She picked up her coat, eyed the picture once again, and followed him into the living room. "And yours?"

"Once I figured out a way of cutting our below-the-line expenses, it was rapturous. Feel like some coffee?"

"I'll put it on," she offered, wondering why he seemed to avoid looking at her.

But he did watch her as she walked to the kitchen, trying to find some hint of her feelings after having spent the evening with Jed—but he saw nothing different, no look of guilt, no look of ecstasy.

"Where'd you two eat?" he called out.

"Box Tree."

A shrill whistle and then: "What'd you have?"

"Mousse de saumon fumé."

"La-di-da!"

"What did you have for dinner, Steve?"

"Mousse de leftover spaghetti."

"I should have brought you a doggie bag. It was delicious, and that stained-glass paneling is gorgeous." She came into the living room. "Be ready in a minute."

Steve sat on one end of the sofa, and Cathy kicked her shoes off and curled up at the other end.

"So," she said, wanting to make conversation, "another day in the lives of two successful TV producers. What else did you do this evening besides work on the budget?"

Getting up to check the coffee, he said, "I decided to go away for a few days...take a break."

Stunned, Cathy watched him disappear into the kitchen. All she could think about was his ex-wife's picture that had suddenly been put in place in his study.

He came back in. "Coffee's not quite ready."

"Where are you planning to go?"

"Palm Beach...spend some time with Meredith and Robbie."

He was going to her! "When?"

"Probably not until after work on Friday."

"Christmas Eve?" she asked, feeling bewildered and hurt.

"That is Christmas Eve, isn't it?" he commented casually.

"Yes...it is." Her voice was but a whisper. "Kind of sudden, isn't it? The trip, I mean."

"Well...with things going so well at the studio, I guess I just reminded myself that Christmas is the time to be with family." He turned away, hoping she hadn't noticed the jerking motion of his Adam's apple.

"Oh."

"Why don't you take a few days off, C.A.? You're just as bushed as I am. Spend some time with your friend."

"His name is Jed, short for Jack Edward Daugherty."

"Spend some time with Jed. Is he stationed here?"

"No," she said icily.

"Why not have him stay here at the house with you?"

Cathy felt as though he had just thrown cold water in her face.

"You wouldn't mind?" she asked curiously.

"Mind? Hell no. I'd feel a lot better knowing you weren't here alone."

"You're all heart, Steve."

"I am, aren't I?"

She got up quickly. "I'll get the coffee."

After she left, Steve took in a deep breath as he pushed one thumbnail against the other, feeling like Caesar must have felt after he had crossed the Rubicon, after he had set into action an irrevocable plan.

"Thanks," he said softly as Cathy handed him his coffee mug.

"Think nothing of it," she replied coldly. Then, not being able to help it, she asked, "Steve, why don't we have dinner out tomorrow night?"

"Sorry. I've got plans."

Another splash of ice water, but this one was even colder. "Oh...that's too bad." Quickly she calculated that with dinner out on Thursday and with his leaving Friday, she wouldn't see him again until after Christmas. "I'd best give you your present now, then."

She took her coat and went upstairs to get his gift. As she did, Steve went into the study and retrieved a small package from the drawer of his desk.

Cathy seemed to be taking a little longer than he had imagined she would, and when she did come back into the living room, he thought her eyes were a little red.

"Here, Steve. Merry Christmas," she said tonelessly, handing him his package, neatly wrapped in red paper with a decorated Christmas tree on top.

"For you, Cathy."

She took the little package from him.

He waited for her to open it, but she said, "You first."

"That's pretty," he said, admiring the tree. Then, he carefully opened his gift.

Pinned to a pair of baby blue Jockey shorts was a heavy gold chain with an "I love New York" symbol dangling from it.

"That's nice," he murmured.

"To go with your T-shirt. I thought it was appropriate since you seem to be nuts about the place."

Fingering the chain, he replied, "I guess I am. Some people just see the seamy side, but there's a lot more to it."

"Like sunsets at Battery Park?" she asked bitterly.

"Something like that." His voice had lost all its musicality. "Aren't you going to open yours?"

She did and in a little velvet box she found a delicate gold bracelet, a miniature gold TV camera hanging securely from it. She saw *C.A.* inscribed on the top side of the camera.

"Turn it over," he said.

On the other side she saw, *Love, S.B.*

Quickly she brushed her eyelid. "We would have had a nice Christmas morning, wouldn't we have, Steve?"

"I couldn't exchange it, Cathy. . .not after having it engraved," he apologized.

She just stared at him, and then said, "Why would you want to exchange it?"

He got up, paced a bit with his hands dug into his pockets. Then he walked to the fireplace, rested his arm on it and turned to face her. "I know about Jed, Cathy. . .and your son."

She sat frozen, feeling faint as the blood drained from her face. Slowly she laid her gift from him on the sofa and then folded her hands, hands that felt like ice, although the room was quite warm. Her vision seemed to become hazy; her lips quivered slightly.

"It's extraordinary how we women try to keep our little secrets, secrets that can't really be kept," she whispered.

"Why did you think it had to be a secret?" he asked, not really understanding.

Still half dazed, she answered, "Well, it's not a secret anymore, is it?"

"Cathy, I wish I could take back that remark I made to you about your never having lost a son"—he pounded the mantel with his fist—"but it's too late for that. I'm just so damn sorry I said it."

"Cheer up, Steve." Her voice rang with false gaiety. "It's almost Christmas. . .a time for laughter and fun, and I hope you have fun in Palm Beach. I know how much you like the sun. Maybe you'll even get a chance to walk in the rain."

She picked up her gift and started toward the staircase. Steve gently took hold of her arm.

"I guess we never do know when a miracle is going to happen, do we, Cathy?"

She looked at him, confusion obvious in her eyes. "A miracle. . .what miracle?"

"It's a miracle that you and Jed have crossed paths again. . .that you've gotten back together."

So that's what you want! she thought, feeling as though a whirlwind was playing havoc with her brain.

Steve let go of her arm, raked his fingers through his dark waves. "I've been vain, Cathy. . .very vain. I've even thought that maybe you and I—" His laugh was low and painful. "You have no idea how many ways a vain man can torture himself."

If the whirlwind in her head had subsided, if she hadn't been so preoccupied with the conclusion that she had drawn—her thinking that Steve wanted her and Jed to be together—Cathy might have heard what he was saying, what he was admitting, but her thoughts were in such turmoil that she wasn't even listening. All her brain registered was that he wanted Jed to have her.

"Yes," she finally said, her voice mechanical, "it is like a miracle, isn't it?" Then she went upstairs to her room.

Steve watched her for a moment and then rushed to the door leading to the deck at the rear of the house. He threw it open and dashed out into the cold night air. The temperature had dropped to below freezing. He felt his skin tingle, felt the cold air surge into his nostrils, grab his ears, and he was relieved—relieved because for a moment he had thought he would never feel anything ever again.

Chapter Fourteen

All day Thursday, Cathy and Steve walked on eggs whenever their paths crossed. Purposefully, she let him know that she was meeting Jed in the plaza downstairs after work, information that seemed to turn him ashen.

That afternoon, Holly took Cathy aside.

"Listen, Cathy, I know you don't mean to be a Scrooge, but you're doing a great job of ruining Steve's Christmas."

"Steve's Christmas? What about mine? And I thought you were *my* friend."

"I am your friend, and I'm Steve's, too. If his mouth drops any lower, he's going to scrape that gorgeous chin of his on the floor."

"I am not my brother's keeper, Holly."

"*You* need a keeper!" she blurted out firmly, but in hushed tones. "Jed pops up in your life again and you turn your back on the greatest man God ever made."

Cathy leaned against the wall outside of Steve's secretary's office, nervously tapping her pen against her clipboard.

"Holly, Jed asked me to marry him last night," she said quietly, without the excitement one would expect.

"He's a little late, isn't he? About fourteen years too late."

"I was in love with Jed once, Holly."

"Cathy, honey," Holly said softly, "marrying him now is not going to make what you two did years ago any more respectable. It's not going to change anything that happened, anything you went through. And what about Steve?"

"What about him?" Her voice was tinged with bitterness.

"He's crazy about you. Don't you know he's in love with you?"

"If he were, why would he want Jed and me to get together again?"

"Did Steve tell you that?" Her voice was doubting.

"In so many words, he did. He even suggested that Jed stay with me at the house while he's away. He wants to spend Christmas with his ex-wife and his son in Palm Beach. He's leaving tomorrow. Her husband is in Europe again."

"Tomorrow? He just said good-bye to me a few minutes ago and wished me a Merry Christmas."

"Good-bye?" Cathy repeated, her thoughts racing wildly.

"Yes, and speaking of good-byes, did you ever think that maybe you're so wrapped up in the good-byes you've received, so wrapped up that you aren't even aware of the good-bye you're dishing out to Steve?"

"Are you sure he was leaving today?"

"Check with his secretary. And Cathy—open your eyes, please."

Holly was the second person to tell her to open her eyes, and now Cathy began to wonder if she hadn't been seeing things all that clearly.

"Terry," she asked, walking into the secretary's office, "is Steve coming back today?"

The dark-haired girl looked up at her. "Today? No, Cathy, he's gone. Won't be back until next Wednesday. In fact, I changed his reservations for him to tonight. His plane leaves at ten-fifteen this evening."

Cathy checked her watch—almost five-thirty, and she was to meet Jed at six o'clock.

"Thanks, Terry."

She closed the door and went back to her office, fighting the heavy pain she felt in her chest. She picked up the phone, punched a few numbers, then quickly hung up.

A little after six, Cathy waited for Jed on the Fifth Avenue side of Rockefeller Center. As she looked down into the lower level, the laughter and smiles of the ice skaters created a sharp contrast to her own feeling of depression, a depression that worsened as she gazed around at the Christmas plants in the Channel, the flower-lined promenade between the buildings leading to the RCA Building.

What was it she had told Steve? she tried to recall—that Christmas was a time for laughter, a time for fun. Why was it, she mused, that she didn't feel at all like laughing, that life was not really that much fun?

Why was it that with the cold wind blowing violently across her face, she was thinking of a blazing sunset on a hot August evening, of bagels and lox, of Oktoberbust?

She gathered her fur collar closer around her cheeks with her gloved hands, but the coldness she felt didn't come from the chill of the wind, it came from within her heart. Why would Steve have told her he was leaving Friday and then slip away so suddenly, as if he were trying to avoid her? she asked herself, but no answer came.

Holly had said he loved her, but if he did why was he making it so convenient for her and Jed to be together, to actually be alone in Steve's own home?

Open your eyes, Holly had told her, and she recalled Steve having told her the same thing. Was she blind to a reality that everyone else saw? Did she love Steve so much that she would be willing to risk being hurt again? And was she, as Holly said, dishing out a final good-bye to him?

The carolers began "I Wonder as I Wander out under the Stars." Cathy looked up to the sky, at the faraway scintillations that had become brighter as darkness set in. How distant they seemed, and how infinitesimal she suddenly felt, how unimportant life had become, knowing that Steve— "Catherine!"

She turned to see Jed walking quickly toward her.

"Sorry I'm late. The traffic is crazy."

"Rush hour plus Christmas shoppers," she said.

Jed looked across the plaza to the huge tree covered with lights. "Isn't that something? Really puts you in the spirit, doesn't it? I love Christmas." He looked at her with soft gray eyes. "And this one is so very special."

Cathy couldn't look back at him. Instead she gazed at the crimson poinsettias, seeing only a crimson sunset, and when Jed's arm reached around her shoulder, she knew it was not the arm that held her that August evening—the feel was different, the touch not as special.

"Catherine, have you thought it over? About marrying me?" he asked hopefully.

Now she did look up at his handsome face, picturing him without his mustache, seeing him as the eighteen-year-old boy she would have died for.

"Jed," she said suddenly, "kiss me."

"Now? Here?"

"Kiss me, Jed!" she insisted.

He looked around awkwardly and then took her in his arms and kissed her softly at first, and then ardently. The kiss completed, he held her at arm's length, his mouth forming a questioning smile, but his smile evaporated when Cathy took a step back from him, causing his arms to fall aimlessly at his sides.

"Good-bye, Jed," she said with finality and walked hurriedly away.

At the curb, Cathy hailed cab after cab. Finally one stopped. She looked at her watch—almost six-thirty. Would Steve have left yet? A feeling of panic shot through her.

The trip to the Village seemed to take an eternity; the light snow that had begun to fall did little to help the already snarled traffic, but finally it pulled up in front of the town house on St. Luke's Place.

Inside, Steve was holding his overcoat and was just about to pick up his suitcase when he heard the front door close. Quickly he shoved his suitcase behind the sofa.

"Steve!" Cathy called as she rushed into the living room. Seeing him, she stopped. Then, with relief in her voice, she said, "I wasn't sure you'd be here."

"I was just leaving. I wasn't really expecting you," he said nervously. "I thought you and Jed would be..." He tossed his overcoat across the back of the sofa. "Together. Did you come home to change?"

Cathy looked into the mirror. From where she was standing she could see his suitcase hidden behind the sofa. "Yes, I'm going to change," she said enigmatically. Looking at the dark three-piece suit he was wearing, she went on, "You look nice. A date?"

Absentmindedly his hands brushed across his vest. "Uh...no, not exactly."

Without even removing her coat or fur hat, she went to the bar cart and poured two glasses of Calvados. "Do you have time for a Christmas drink?" she asked, handing him the glass.

"I guess so, but I have to be leaving soon, Cathy."

"I see," she said casually, taking off her hat and coat and sitting across from him, her legs crossed gracefully.

He sat down on the sofa. "How is Jed?"

"Fine...full of the Christmas spirit."

"Good...that's good," he commented dryly. "I imagine he's a nice guy."

"Very nice." She watched him sip his brandy. "In fact, he's asked me to marry him."

This time he took a big sip, and then, hoarsely, he remarked, "Life does fulfill some of our dreams, doesn't it?"

"Some, Steve," she answered, her voice still so-so.

"When's the happy event?"

"You mean, when do I plan to get married?" She saw him wince.

"Yes." His voice was more a sigh, and then he forced a weak smile.

"Are you smiling because you're glad, sad, or mad, Steve? I'm never quite certain."

"Cathy, if you're happy, how could I be anything but glad?" he answered sincerely.

She took his empty glass from him. "You're such a sport."

He leaned back on the sofa, laid his arm across the back of it, and began tapping his fingers. "Well, I never thought of it that way, but I guess you're right." He checked his watch. "You didn't say when you were getting married."

"Not until I've had one last fling," she told him, handing him his glass.

Silence.

"Take your glass, Steve," she suggesting, enjoying the shocked look on his face.

"One last fling?" he repeated in amazement.

"Yes. Why not? Men have their bachelor parties, and I assume my husband-to-be will have his. Why can't I have one?"

Steve tugged at his earlobe. "Why not!"

"And you're invited, Steve." Her smile was purity itself.

"Cathy...are you thinking I'm going to jump out of a cake or something?"

"Or something."

Suspiciously: "What are you up to, C.A.?"

She leaned back in her chair and held her glass up to the light as though to examine it. "Picture this scenario, Steve.

A woman is about to give up her freedom...no more paramours. This woman wants one more memory to take with her before she says 'I do.' Now, don't you think she deserves it, just as any man would tell you he does?''

"If you're asking me if I support the double standard...I don't.''

Cathy leaned forward. "Well then, Steve, how about a little walk down memory lane?''

Putting his glass down, he snapped, "I don't think you're talking about walking!'' He jumped up. "This may come as a surprise to you, Miss Modern, but I'm really a very old-fashioned guy.''

"You're not old, Steve.''

"I'm forty.''

"The red wine of youth is gushing in your veins.''

"Cathy...have you been drinking?''

"No, but you have the same heady effect on me.'' Now she stood up. "You're a very provocative man, Steve.''

His eyes narrowed as he looked at a Cathy he had never known before. "I'm really quite dull.''

She took a step toward him. "You're exciting.''

Backing away, he said, "My nose is crooked.''

She followed. "You're desirable.''

Another step backward. "I eat crackers in bed.''

Closer to him, she teased, "I'll give you something better to do in bed.''

Cathy had backed him to the sofa and his body fell heavily onto it.

"What's gotten into you, C.A.?''

She sat down beside him and began to unbutton his vest. "I just want a piece of the action...that's all.''

He pushed her fingers away and began to rebutton his vest. "Why do I wish Jed were here?" he said to himself as he got up, faced the fireplace, and spread his arms out, resting his hands on the mantel. Then, he turned. "Cathy, I think you've gone off the deep end."

"Why do you say that, S.B.?"

"Listen." He shook his finger at her. "I'm the one who's supposed to have the weird sense of humor."

"It's not weird, Steve. In fact, I've gotten used to it. I look forward to it." Crossing her legs, she began a sultry swinging motion with her dangling leg.

"This isn't happening," he said to the mantel.

"But it's going to, Steve. Trust me," she added, using one of his favorite phrases.

"Catherine Arensen," he started, looking her straight in the eye, "are you suggesting that you and I...that we...tonight...now?"

"Hang in there with that thought, Steve."

In amazement, he watched her go to the front door, heard her slam the bolt in place. Returning to the living room, she went to the stereo and inserted the Rachmaninoff tape.

"I'll be right back, S.B." She took her coat and started up the stairway. Halfway up, she turned to him, smiled, and put her hand to her throat delicately. "Don't you dare leave...not yet."

Steve swallowed hard and caught himself smiling; he waved his hand in front of his eyes. "Whoa, boy...whoa! Get a hold on yourself. It's a fabulous going-away present, but...but what? Hell, I'm no iceberg!"

Hurriedly he grabbed his suitcase and hid it under the desk in the study. Returning, he refilled both their glasses and waited, his mind feverishly anticipating her coming downstairs.

And when she did, Steve's eyes opened in wonderment.

Cathy glided down the stair in a new coral negligee, her makeup fresh, her loose hair shiny and silky, her hazel eyes flaring their green hue. For a moment she paused at the bottom of the staircase and rested her hand on the railing. The glimmer of the bracelet he had given her caught his eye. Then, glancing at the alluring negligee, she saw him bite his lower lip.

"Uh. . .is that outfit new?" he asked, thinking only that she must have dipped into her trousseau.

"Yes. Like it?" She stepped onto the carpet and turned gracefully, holding the edges of the robe, letting it flow softly as she turned. "I wanted to look my best when you decided to send me to Jed."

The sound of that name dampened his spirits. "I told you to invite him here. I didn't say I would like it."

"Oh? Second thoughts?" she asked, floating past him.

He scanned every curve of her body that the molded gown would permit, his eyes settling on the low-cut lace-work at her breasts.

"Second and third," he admitted. Then, checking his three-piece suit, he asked, "Why do I feel overdressed?"

"Because you are." She sidled up next to him and began removing his jacket. "But we can take care of that."

He let her take the jacket off him. After tossing it on the sofa on top of his overcoat, she again started on the buttons of his vest.

"I can do that," he protested.

"No," she said quickly, "I'm enjoying it."

The vest followed the jacket and then she slowly undid his tie, watching the whites of his eyes grow larger and larger.

"That does feel better," he said, smiling uncomfortably, and then jumping as Cathy pulled the tails of his shirt from inside his pants. His laugh was forced. "You do that so well."

"You know what I really think, Steve? I think you should slip into something more comfortable...like your cute little brown robe."

"My robe?"

"And why don't you put on the chain I gave you."

"Your chain."

"Yes...*just* my chain and your robe."

For the second time that night he swallowed hard. "Just the chain and the robe."

"Steve, are you going to repeat everything I say all evening?"

"Oh...no...no."

"Besides, I know how much you hate feeling confined when you're relaxing at home."

Awkwardly, Steve gathered up his strewn clothes, an odd smile on his mouth, his brown eyes glowing. Hearing her call his name, he turned to see her leaning over the back of the sofa, leaning low.

"Why don't you put on some of that lime after-shave of yours, too."

Cathy couldn't help but smile as she watched him bound up the stairs two at a time.

Now it was her turn to wait, but not for long.

Steve started down the stairs at a good pace, but seeing Cathy sitting on the sofa, looking very relaxed, he slowed to a reasonable speed.

He stood at the bottom of the staircase and apologized. "Sorry I took so long."

Cathy eyes started at his firm ankles and moved ever so slowly up his long, strong legs, upward over his short robe, not missing his well-formed arms. Her gaze settled at his throat. "That chain looks good on you." Then her eyes rose to meet his and they stayed there until he looked away.

"Yes, it's very nice. Thank you again. The bracelet looks good on you, too."

She held her arm straight up in the air, moving her wrist so the chain sparkled, letting the soft silk of the sleeve of her negligee fall away. "It is lovely, isn't it?"

Looking at her lacy bodice: "Just lovely."

"Have a seat, Steve." She patted the cushion next to her on the sofa.

He picked up his brandy and started for the other side of the room.

"Steve," she said with music in her voice as she patted the sofa again, "it's *my* party."

Cautiously he walked back and sat down, adjusting his robe very carefully.

"Now," she said, "isn't this nice? But you look nervous." She moved closer to him and put her hand on his wrist, and then moved her fingers slowly and caressingly upward across his forearm, under the rim of the robe's three-quarter-length sleeve, upward still, pushing the material as her fingers strayed to his shoulder and rubbed it soothingly. "I hope you're not overexcited about anything."

His only response was a low moan of delight at her touch.

Cathy let her heeled slippers fall to the carpet and then curled up close to him. As she placed her left arm across the sofa in back of him, she laid her other hand on his chest.

"Your heart is beating erratically, Steve." She saw his Adam's apple bob. "Do you think you're coming down with something?" She ran her fingertips gently over his knee, slipped them under his robe and began featherlike strokes across his thigh. "You do seem to be warm all over."

He lunged forward and dashed to the kitchen, mumbling, "It's just that I haven't eaten...and the brandy. I need something to snack on."

While Steve had been changing, Cathy had switched to the FM station, and now the soothing music was punctuated with noises from the kitchen.

"What are you doing in there?" she called to him.

"Got something in the microwave," he called back.

She knew he was stalling for time, and she knew exactly what she was doing. She loved Steve and would never let him go. And she was enjoying making him nervous, enjoying postponing the moment when she would tell him she had no intention of marrying Jed or any other man— except him.

Finally he came back in carrying two small plates and two napkins. Spreading one over her lap, he handed her a dish and sat down next to her.

"What're these?" She looked at the large puffed squares of something. Then she sniffed at them.

"A knish," he said, as though she should have known.

"Oh...a knish." Now it was her turn to start repeating him. "What's a knish?"

"Kind of like baked mashed potatoes," he told her.

"Baked mashed potatoes?"

"Sure. They're delicious. Taste it."

"Knish. . .not very romantic." She bit off a small piece. "Tastes good, though," she admitted.

"Didn't think you'd had time for dinner." He finished his first knish and started on his second. "You haven't lived until you've had them at Coney Island. . .they sell them right there on the beach. And Nathan's hot dogs. . .boy oh boy!"

"Steve, you must have a cast-iron stomach."

Having finished his second knish, he looked over at her plate. "Not going to eat that one?"

She held the plate toward him and he took the knish. "Why do I feel you've just put a damper on my party?" she asked suspiciously.

Chewing zestfully, he glanced over at her. "Didn't mean to, but we do have to eat, you know. Remember what happened to you the first night you were here. . .you fell asleep."

"Yes, and I woke up to bagels and lox."

"Eat," he ordered, wanting her to finish her knish. "You've got to keep your strength up."

"What for?"

"The honeymoon," he said sharply.

She sank her teeth into the knish.

Steve put his plate on the table and picked up his brandy glass. Leaning back, he stretched his legs, crossing them at the ankles, watching her peck at the baked mashed potatoes. Next he lit a cigarette and exhaled a smooth stream of smoke.

"Does Jed like bagels?"

"I don't know," she answered matter-of-factly, shrugging her shoulders.

"Does he sing in the shower?"

"I'm not sure."

"Cook?"

"How would I know? I haven't seen him for fourteen years!"

He pulled one end of his robe over the other. "You sure don't know very much about the guy you're going to marry, do you?"

"You never do *really* know a man until you've lived with him."

"Boy," he moaned, "you know how to hurt a guy!"

"What? I just said—"

"That I didn't measure up...that's what you implied."

"That's what you inferred," she corrected, handing him her empty plate.

"Well, tell me C.A., what was so bad about living with me?"

"S.B., do knishes always make you so sensitive, or are you just trying to pick a fight with me, trying to ruin my party?"

He angled a quizzical look at her. "You really want to go through with this, Cathy?"

Now she wasn't so sure. When she had had him on the run, she'd thought it was a fun game, but the look in his eyes now told her he was seriously contemplating making love to her.

Suddenly she was furious. *How could he?* she asked herself, *how dare he even consider taking me to bed, thinking he would then turn me over to another man!* Getting up from the sofa, she stalked to the easy chair across from him.

Instinctively knowing the ball was now in his court, Steve smiled to himself, partly because he saw again the familiar Cathy leering at him from across the room, and partly because he felt more comfortable chasing than he did being chased. "I don't know why you're so upset," he said innocently.

"I'm not upset."

"You certainly act like you are."

"I'm *not* upset," she repeated.

"Good. Now we can get back to your little arrangement, then."

"What arrangement?"

"Your. . .what did you call it?" He hadn't forgotten. "Oh, yes...your one last fling." He stretched out on the sofa, his palms under his head. "A little walk down memory lane."

"Cover yourself!" she told him, looking toward the fireplace.

"Oops." He pulled his robe over his thighs. "I hope Jed knows what he's getting into."

Disgruntled, she snapped, "I don't think we should be talking about Jed right now!"

"That's understandable." He angled a glance at her. "Does he have any idea about this...fling of yours?"

"I didn't ask his permission, if that's what you mean." Why was it she felt the whole idea was beginning to backfire on her?

"Good. I'd begin to worry about him if he did. Not that I wouldn't think he was one helluva guy if he did know and—"

"Steve—"

"Oh, is it time?"

"Time for what?"

"The party."

"Steven Bronsky"—she stood up, looking elegant in her coral negligee—"for your information, the party's over!"

"But it hasn't even begun yet." He got up from the sofa, went to her, and held her arms out to her sides. "Look at you. . .all dressed up." His arms slid around her waist. "And you smell so good. You know, it makes me feel really special that you did all this just for me. . .that you chose me to have your last fling with."

The pressure of his hands at her back, his gentle forcing her against his body, the whiff of his lime fragrance—everything about him made her automatically move her arms to his shoulders, to the soft velour of his robe.

"Steve, I—"

"No more talk, Cathy."

The next instant she felt his lips on hers, his soft, warm mouth brushing against hers, his tongue tracing her lips; then his lips moved across her cheek, up to her eyelids, down to the tip of her nose and then back again to her mouth, but this time she felt his arms wrap around her tightly as his tongue forced its way past her lips.

At that moment, his holding her was everything she ever wanted in the world, everything she had ever dreamed of, waited for. The warmth of his body, the strength of his arms about her, the knowledge that he wanted her caused her knees to turn to jelly, so deliriously happy did she feel.

She slouched against him and he supported her with his chest. Nuzzling into his neck, she kissed him and slid one hand inside the open collar of his robe, letting her fingertips brush across his hard chest muscles, tingling as they slid through the softness of the fine hairs.

She felt the kiss he placed on her head as his hands massaged her back. One hand slipped up into his wavy hair as the other slid from his chest down to the firm muscles of his side.

"Steve," she whispered, "why were you leaving tonight instead of tomorrow?"

"Why are you going to marry Jed?" he whispered back, nibbling at her earlobe.

"I never intended to," she admitted, her eyes closed, her entire body alive at the feel of him. "I said good-bye to him this evening."

"You what?" she heard him right in her ear. Then, holding her away from him: "And you let me think—"

She looked up into his wide eyes. "Don't be angry with me...please don't."

"Angry?" He held her close. "How could I be angry with someone I love so much? Even though you are a little strange."

"And you're not?" she asked, snuggling against him again, feeling his hands create trails of fire over her shoulders and back, feeling the excitement of his firm thighs pressing into hers.

"I guess we do deserve each other, don't we?" He leaned down and kissed her throat, working his mouth downward. Then, leaning back from her, he looked into her shining eyes. "Now, about this party—"

"It's off," she said sorrowfully. "Remember, I'm not getting married."

"Oh, yes you are. How does Mrs. Steven Bronsky sound to you?"

Again her legs weakened. "Steve...are you sure?"

"Cathy, I've never been more sure of anything in my life. Besides, do you think I could sleep nights with you running loose in Manhattan?"

She felt herself being swooped up in Steve's strong arms and he started up the stairs.

"Well, C.A., it's party time."

Chapter Fifteen

As Steve carried Cathy higher up the stairs, her heart soared to even greater heights. *Mrs. Steven Bronsky*, her heart echoed, and she reveled in the thought of it.

Once inside his bedroom, he gently set her down.

"Now that I've carried you over the threshold, it's just about official," he said softly as they stood together in the darkness of the room.

Cathy leaned against him, her hands touching his. "Our loving each other makes it more than official."

"And I do love you, Cathy...so very much."

The silk robe of her negligee rippled down her arms as he slipped it from her shoulders; she watched as he laid it across the chair by the window and then removed his own robe, carefully placing it next to hers.

Her pulse quickened as his hand pushed back the sheer panels.

With his strong back to her, Steve moved his arms up high against the window frame, the moonlight outlining in gold his dark muscular form.

"How beautiful the moon is when you're in love," he said, his voice low and musical.

Quietly, Cathy stepped across the thick carpet and stood next to him, putting her arm around his waist. "Look, you can see his eyes and his mouth," she said, looking up at the man in the moon.

"Know why he's smiling, love?"

"Why?" she asked, leaning back against the window frame, looking over at Steve, her heart beginning to flutter joyously as she watched the moonlight bathing his body in golden light.

"He's smiling because he sees how happy we are...how right everything is for us."

Then, sliding his strong hands up her arms to her shoulders, his fingers brushed aside the straps of her gown. It felt to her like the delicate glissando of a soft harp as the silky material slipped from her body, and now the moonlight painted them both in golden hues.

"You're beautiful, Mrs. Bronsky," he whispered as his eyes caressed her, hungrily searching out every curvature and indention of her feminine form.

Cathy's hands rose to his chest and then moved up to his broad shoulders, her fingers trembling slightly at the touch of him. "And you're beautiful, Mr. Bronsky."

Steve slouched back against his side of the window frame, his eyes never leaving her, but as though in quiet reverie he gazed at the firm softness of her breasts. She saw his lips quiver ever so slightly as his gaze lowered to that place that felt to her like a lotus flower trembling to bloom.

Then, with a golden glow in his eyes, he extended his arms to her.

Like a small ship entering the safety of a peaceful harbor, she moved into his welcoming embrace, glorying in the touch of him, the warmth of his body, the strength of his arms.

The feel of his warm flesh was exciting as her hands slid around his waist and he drew her closer against him. Laying her head on his shoulder she kissed his neck, let her tongue dally on his skin, delighting in the delicate salty taste of him as she inhaled the faint aroma of lime on his cheek. Her totally alive senses sent a sudden shiver running across her skin. Steve felt her quiver.

"What is it, love? Are you cold?"

"No, it's not that," she said, holding on to him tightly. "I just had an awful feeling that I'm too happy for it to last."

Comfortingly, he moved his hands across her back and shoulders. "It will last. As long as we have breath in us, it will last."

She lifted her head from its resting place and looked up into his tranquil face. "I want it to...I want it to so much."

Her eyes told him of her concern. Putting his arm around her, he guided her toward the bed. In one swoop he turned down the coverlet. Then sitting on the side of the bed, he drew her to him; as she stood before him, he put his arms around her, kissed her abdomen and laid his cheek against it.

"I'll always be right next to you, Cathy, to hold you, to make you feel secure, to let you know you're loved."

She felt the slight roughness of the stubble of his beard as he pressed his face across her stomach; the roughness was immediately replaced by the tenderness of the kisses he taunted her with as he slowly moved downward.

With one hand on his shoulder to steady herself, she guided the other through his hair as she trembled with delight at the searchings of his tongue, at the soothing massaging his hands were working at her buttocks, down farther across the back of her legs—legs that were fast becoming too weak to hold her securely. Her quiverings escalated as did her moans of pleaure. Her heart palpitating wildly, she pleaded, ''Promise me, Steve...promise me we'll never have to say good-bye.''

Placing his face on her soft skin, he assured her. ''I promise. With all my heart, I promise.'' Along his cheek he felt her breath begin to syncopate. Looking up at her he could see the glistening at her eyelids. He slid over on the bed and put his hand out to her. ''Come here, love.''

Cathy slipped down beside him; he took her in his arms, cuddling her, running his warm hand across her arm and hip.

''We're supposed to be happy. Why the tears?''

She pressed her palm into the soft skin of his back. ''I told you once before...women sometimes cry whey they're happy. Don't you remember?''

His laugh was deep, yet soft. ''Yes, and I still don't understand why.'' He kissed her forehead. ''You're going to have to let me know when you're crying because you're happy and when you're crying because you're sad. Deal?''

''A deal,'' she agreed, now moving her hand across his firm thigh, her fingertips digging into his solid muscles.

Gently he swung her on top of him as though she were light as a feather. With his legs spread slightly, her own slipped in between his and she felt them close against hers.

"You know what, C.A.?"

"What?" she asked softly.

"I love you."

At the realization of his excitement, a wild tingling sensation surged across her stomach. Folding her arms across his chest, Cathy lifted her head up so she could see him. The moonlight was doing fabulous things to the sheen of his bronzed skin; an easy breeze outside caused the shadows of the leafless branches of a tree to dance across his face.

While her fingertips traced the outline of his lips and chin, Cathy smiled. "And I love you, S.B."

"That does make it nice for us, doesn't it?" he told her as he began his easy undulations, as the pressure of his strong hands forced her body against his thighs.

As she leaned down to brush kisses across his chest, flicking her tongue teasingly at his hardened nipples, her hands reached for his strong arms, thrilling in the power of his biceps.

"Ah, Cathy," he whispered contentedly, "I love it when you touch me, when you stroke me. Your hands are so soft."

Gently he rolled her onto her back next to him. Raising himself onto one elbow, his hand propping up his head, he watched the moonlight streaming across her body, his eyes absorbing the alabaster glow of her skin.

"I never get tired of looking at you, and everytime I do I see something more wonderful about you."

His free hand slid over one breast and then the other, his thumb gently circling the aureoles, kneading her taut rosebuds. She shuddered as she felt his warm mouth move from one breast to the other, as she felt his moist tongue lap at her hardened tips.

Cathy's head tilted back on the pillow as she sank into the wonderment of her new world, a world made beautiful and loving by the man at her breast, by the very feel of him. For a moment her fear that it could not possibly last gripped her again, but then his words echoed in her heart: *I'll always be right next to you, Cathy, to hold you, to make you feel secure, to let you know you're loved.*

She was so full of happiness and contentment that she wanted to shout it out to the world, to tell everyone that she did feel secure, that she knew she loved and was loved. And she would have given voice to the delightful feelings that were surging through her body, but in the next moment Steve's lips were on hers, his hand running along the inside of her thigh, working its way toward the fire that was again smoldering deep within her, a fire ignited by the feel of his throbbing body.

And then she felt the weight of his warm body as he moved over her, settling on her gently. With hands on either side of her, Steve raised himself slightly; his brown eyes shone with silver as he looked down at her, and then he begged, ''Now, Cathy...please.''

Steve's contented moan filled the room, her own contentment growing as he nibbled at her ear. Then began his easy, powerful motions, movements of love that she accepted with ever-increasing delight.

Her entire body began to move with him and then she began to tense under his wilder thrustings. Loving the feel of the weight of him, her fingers pressed into his back and then slipped downward and dug into his solid buttocks.

"Cathy!" His voice was urgent.

Feeling her body arch upward against the taut muscles of his thighs, Steve pressed his mouth against Cathy's as their wild cries of ecstacy mingled, rushing in unison across their lips as their breathing reached a peak of urgency, as their togetherness burst forth to become the one important reality in their joined existence.

Was it a moment later? Was it an eon? Cathy didn't know. Time was meaningless. All she knew was that she felt Steve's warm panting breath on her breast. Raising her hand, she ran her unsteady fingers across his perspiring brow and through his soft hair.

"Steve," she whispered.

"Umm-hmm," he mumbled.

"Why do I love you so much?"

"What can I tell you?" His voice flowed out in soft contentment. "Maybe it's my cooking."

"You say the dumbest things."

"It's a gift."

Easing her hand across the warm smoothness of his back, she said, "Know what? I think we should go downstairs, have another knish, and then come back up here and see what happens."

"C.A.," he sighed, "you're going to make a youngster out of me yet."

Cathy smiled into the moonlit room, her eyes still closed, her own breathing not yet settled. She could feel the deep thudding of Steve's heartbeat against her chest, and it felt wonderful to her.

"S.B.," she countered, "if you get any younger, you're going to make an old lady out of me."

"So we'll grow old together."

The hands that she felt roaming alongside her hips and legs were warm and soothing. If loving were never again to be as wonderful, she felt she would have enough memories for two lifetimes, but in her heart she knew that loving Steve would only get better with time.

She watched the light of the moon glow on his face as he lifted himself up and gazed down on her; she watched with wonderment the smile that lit up the entire room.

"What day is this?" he asked.

"Friday has just begun...Christmas Eve. Why?"

He rolled over onto his side. "Let's see"—he began to calculate on his fingers—"Friday, Saturday, Sunday, Monday, Tuesday...five days and five nights until we go back to work. Five days and five nights of heaven with you. We'll unplug the phone...won't answer the door." He kissed the palm of her hand. "How does that sound, C.A.?"

"Sounds like heaven, S.B.," she answered, propping herself up on her elbow and kissing him softly.

The Silhouette Cameo Tote Bag Now available for just $6.99

Handsomely designed in blue and bright pink, its stylish good looks make the Cameo Tote Bag an attractive accessory. The Cameo Tote Bag is big and roomy (13″ square), with reinforced handles and a snap-shut top. You can buy the Cameo Tote Bag for $6.99, plus $1.50 for postage and handling.

Send your name and address with check or money order for $6.99 (plus $1.50 postage and handling), a total of $8.49 to:

Silhouette Books
120 Brighton Road
P.O. Box 5084
Clifton, NJ 07015-5084
ATTN: Tote Bag

SIL-T-1

The Silhouette Cameo Tote Bag can be purchased pre-paid only. No charges will be accepted. Please allow 4 to 6 weeks for delivery.

Arizona and N.Y. State Residents Please Add Sales Tax

Offer not available in Canada.

AMERICAN TRIBUTE

Where a man's dreams count for more than his parentage...

Look for these upcoming titles under the Special Edition American Tribute banner.

LOVE'S HAUNTING REFRAIN
Ada Steward #289—February 1986
For thirty years a deep dark secret kept them apart—King Stockton made his millions while his wife, Amelia, held everything together. Now could they tell their secret, could they admit their love?

THIS LONG WINTER PAST
Jeanne Stephens #295—March 1986
Detective Cody Wakefield checked out Assistant District Attorney Liann McDowell, but only in his leisure time. For it was the danger of Cody's job that caused Liann to shy away.

AM-TRIB-1

AMERICAN TRIBUTE

RIGHT BEHIND THE RAIN
Elaine Camp #301—April 1986
The difficulty of coping with her brother's
death brought reporter Raleigh Torrence
to the office of Evan Younger, a police
psychologist. He helped her to deal with
her feelings and emotions, including love.

CHEROKEE FIRE
Gena Dalton #307—May 1986
It was Sabrina Dante's silver spoon that
Cherokee cowboy Jarod Redfeather couldn't
trust. The two lovers came from opposite
worlds, but Jarod's Indian heritage taught
them to overcome their differences.

NOBODY'S FOOL
Renee Roszel #313—June 1986
Everyone bet that Martin Dante and Cara
Torrence would get together. But Martin
wasn't putting any money down, and Cara
was out to prove that she was nobody's fool.

MISTY MORNINGS, MAGIC NIGHTS
Ada Steward #319—July 1986
The last thing Carole Stockton wanted was to
fall in love with another politician, especially
Donnelly Wakefield. But under a blanket of
secrecy, far from the campaign spotlights,
their love became a powerful force.

AM-TRIB-1

COMING NEXT MONTH

STATE SECRETS—Linda Lael Miller
When David joined Holly Llewellyn's cooking class, they found themselves instantly attracted to each other, but neither of them could chance falling in love since both had something to hide.

DATELINE: WASHINGTON—Patti Beckman
Investigative reporters Janelle Evans and Bart Tagert had different methods for finding facts, so when they were assigned to the same story the clashes were inevitable…but the passion was unexpected.

ASHES OF THE PAST—Monica Barrie
Although four years had passed since Blair had been widowed, she was reluctant to become involved, until she met author Sean Mathias and a mysterious passion drew her to him.

STRING OF PEARLS—Natalie Bishop
Devon had once believed the worst of Brittany, now the past was repeating itself. Brought together again by the pursuit of a smuggler, could they find the love they had lost?

LOVE'S PERFECT ISLAND—Rebecca Swan
Alex Gilbert and Ian McLeod were on opposing sides of a wildlife issue, until the beauty of the Aleutian Islands lured them away from their debate and into each other's arms.

DEVIL'S GAMBIT—Lisa Jackson
When Zane appeared at Rhodes Breeding Farm insisting that Tiffany's champion stallion was alive, she had to discover if this alluring man was trying to help her, or was seeking revenge.

AVAILABLE NOW: